Snowbirds Pathfinder Club

SANDWICH ISLAND SUMMER

SANDWICH ISLAND SUMMER

COLLEEN L. REECE

REVIEW AND HERALD® PUBLISHING ASSOCIATION
HAGERSTOWN, MD 21740

Copyright © 1991 by Review and Herald® Publishing Association

Originally published by Baker Book House under the title
The Summer of Peter and Pam

The author assumes full responsibility for the accuracy of all facts
and quotations as cited in this book.

This book was
Edited by Richard W. Coffen
Designed by Bill Kirstein / Lee Cherry
Cover Illustration: Scott Snow
Type set: 11.5 pt. Windsor Old Style

PRINTED IN U.S.A.

96 95 94 93 92 91   10 9 8 7 6 5 4 3 2 1

R&H Cataloging Service

Reece, Colleen L.
   Sandwich Island summer.

   I. Title.
    244

ISBN 0-8280-0664-4

Dedication

For the Jim Chapman family,
whose caring for one another,
especially the love between "Peter and Pam,"
contributed much to this story

Contents

Also by Colleen L. Reece

Comrades of the Trail
Escape From Fear
A Gold Star for Eric
Julie's Three Special Letters
JumpStart!
Last Page in the Diary
More Than Confetti
The Mysterious Treadle Machine
P.K. the Great
Plain, Plain Melissa Jane

Chapter One

Pam's pen flew across the paper. "The beautiful girl heard racing footsteps behind her. Running faster, she looked back. The spy had found her out! She must escape. The secret she carried . . ."

"Pam."

Oh, no, not now! Why did Mom need her just this moment? If she left the story she was writing, she might not be able to get back into it later.

"Pam, come here."

With a sigh, Pam dropped the pen. When Katharine Jones called like that it meant *now*. Running her hand through her short blonde hair, Pam went downstairs.

"What do you want, Mom?"

Mrs. Jones's face was serious. "We need to have a little talk, Pam." Pam sighed again and looked out the open window. There had been so many "little talks" since Dad died. She closed her eyes for just a second, trying not to think about Dad. It still hurt too much. When she opened her eyes, Pam saw the look of sympathy on Mom's face, but Mom came straight to the point.

"We're going away for the summer."

"Going away? Where?"

"I've been offered a job cooking at a church boys' camp on Sandwich Island." If a bomb had gone off in their kitchen, Pam wouldn't have been more surprised.

"Cooking! But you're a schoolteacher!"

Mrs. Jones smiled. "I know. But we need the money—what with inflation and all. This is the only thing I could pick up on short notice that would pay well."

"But, Mom! Sandwich Island. Where's *that?*" Pam bit her lip to keep from blurting out her secret, and barely listened as Mom told her about Sandwich Island.

If she noticed the wail in Pam's voice, she ignored it. "Sandwich Island is just north and west of Mount Vernon on Interstate 5, about two hours north of here. Remember the Kincaids? He's the retired Army friend who spends summers cooking for the boys' camp. But it's become too hard a job for him and his wife—they need help. Although they're volunteers, the camp director said they could get someone to help and offer a salary."

Again Pam almost told her secret—that if things went the way she planned, they'd have extra money. But Pam quickly substituted, "You mean we're leaving Seattle—in the summer? I'll miss *everything,* Mom! Our young people's group is going to Seafair, and the Seattle Center, and the docks, and . . ."

Mom was shaking her head. "We're going, Pam. Tomorrow." At her daughter's look of disbelief, she added, "There was no point in telling you until I was sure I could get the job."

Pam just looked at Mom, then away. She felt sick. There went her summer—all the wonderful plans she and Wendy had made, all the fun things! By the time summer was over, Wendy would probably have found another best friend. How could Mom ruin her life like this? Yet deep inside Pam could hear a little voice urging her to be honest with herself. Expenses *had* gone up, terribly. They needed the money. Pam was too young for a summer job. The only thing she had was her secret. If she told Mom *that,* maybe they could stay.

But how could she? How could she tell Mom about those last few minutes before Dad had died? She and Mom had been home when the call came. Dad had been in a head-on collision. He was in the hospital. When they got there, the doctor shook his head. Mr. Jones was hurt badly. The next few hours seemed like a dream, or a horrible nightmare, until the minute when Katharine Jones looked at her husband and saw how weak he was growing. It was during the seconds when she had rushed to the hall for a nurse, that Dad had whispered, "Take care of Mom, Pam." He squeezed her hand as she promised, and the next moment he closed his eyes.

The nurse came in with Mom and picked up Dad's hand. She pushed the button that called "code." Soon Pam could hear the sound of many feet pounding down the hallway. She and Mom nervously passed the next few minutes in the nearby waiting room while the specialists worked over Dad. Finally, the nurse returned. "He's gone." Pam could remember Mom crying. She hadn't cried. She had only felt numb. But that night she thought of her promise to take care of Mom. Just before she fell asleep, she whispered again, "Dad, I'll take care of Mom."

From then on, Pam didn't think about Dad very often. It hurt too much. Once when Mom had tried to tell her that God must have something good in store for them, Pam had rebelled.

"We needed Dad. I don't understand that at all."

But Mom only said quietly, "We aren't always supposed to understand."

No, Pam couldn't tell Mom about those moments, not now, maybe not ever. They were what she had of Dad that belonged just to her. But the frustration of his death, the idea of leaving her friends for the summer, were just too much. Pam forgot she was supposed to be grown-up.

"Just what am I going to do all summer, stuck on some dumb island at a stupid boys' camp, of all places?"

Her mother's voice was stern. "You might try to be of some help. Maybe volunteer to help with the younger boys during staff meetings. There's swimming and hiking. The Kincaids have a boy about your age. His name is Dennis. He's a junior counselor and will show you around. Besides," Mom grinned, "you'll have lots of free time for your writing. Who knows? You may even pick up some ideas!"

Pam just stared. Then she found her voice again. "At a church *boys'* camp? Big chance! This is the summer I . . . I was going to finish my spy story. What can I learn about spies on an island with a bunch of little boys?"

Mom's patience was wearing thin. "Look, Pam, we're going. You should be thanking God I have the chance to earn extra money."

Pam bit her lip. She didn't want to tell Mom how she felt about God since Dad's death. She had avoided everything about God except the church youth group. If Dad hadn't died, Mom wouldn't have had to go back to work. They could have still been a happy family, like they used to be. But Mom was still talking.

"About that spy story—remember what your English teacher wrote on your outline?"

Pam turned red. It wasn't fair for Mom to bring that up. Pam could close her eyes right now and see those awful words that Mrs. Johnstone had written in red ink across the outline: **You have a good way of expressing yourself. Lots of ideas. But you don't know anything about spies and foreign intrigue. It doesn't ring true. Stick with what you know, Pam. You'll get along a lot better.**

Pam had worked hours on that outline. She had

been sure Mrs. Johnstone would approve. Now her chin went up in the air. "After all, Mom, Mrs. Johnstone isn't the only one in the world. Look how many editors turn down books that later become famous!" She caught Mom's smile. "I'm going to finish it. It's a good story. Besides, if I only wrote about what I know, who'd read it?" She mimicked, "Typical teenager from Seattle transplanted to Sandwich Island. Who cares?"

Mom didn't argue. "Typical teenager from Seattle had better get packed. Jeans, slacks, shirts, heavy jacket, swimsuit, a couple of dresses. Even in summer, there's all kinds of weather."

Feeling misunderstood, Pam started for the stairs.

"Don't forget your boots, Pam." *That* was the last straw. Boots! As if she were still a child! Pam gritted her teeth and carefully refrained from slamming the door. But before she started packing, she called Wendy.

"Yes, a boys' camp. On Sandwich Island. Can you imagine anything worse?"

Wendy didn't help a bit. She just giggled. "I can imagine a lot worse things. What age are the boys? Can I go, too?"

Pam hung up with a bang, but Wendy's question stuck with her. Mom had said something about helping with little boys. She had also mentioned a Dennis Kincaid to "show her around." Just what she needed, some drippy boy hanging around all the time!

Tears of anger flooded Pam's eyes as she started throwing things in her suitcases. Why did this have to happen now? Just when Eric Brent had started noticing her? He had moved to their neighborhood a few months earlier, but hadn't paid any attention to her. He was in senior high, dark, with his own car. Then just last week—Pam dropped the jeans she had been folding, remembering what happened.

It must have been the new blue sweater. She looked a lot older than almost 13 in it. Fourteen, maybe. Eric had stopped his car as she got off the school bus. She had stood on the corner talking with him for a few minutes. He was full of excitement over being on the football team at Hillcrest High. She was a good listener, and before Eric drove off he said, "Say, Pam, why don't we get together this summer? I'll call you next week."

Pam's heart wouldn't stay still. Eric Brent call *her?* It was all she could do to answer, "That would be nice." The next minute he was gone.

Pam hadn't mentioned this to Mom. Mom had some pretty old-fashioned ideas about Wendy and her being too young to like boys, especially older boys. But every time the phone rang, Pam's heart shot to her throat. Of all the luck. To be on some island when Eric called! Maybe she should write him a note. A chill went through her. Write to Eric Brent? She tossed her head. Why not? He had said he'd call.

I'll do it first thing when I get to Sandwich Island, Pam promised herself as she jammed more clothes into the suitcase. *At least I have that to look forward to. There won't be anything else exciting up there. Besides, maybe he'll write back.*

Pam was very quiet all evening, and Mom wisely said no more. They went to bed early, but Pam stared out into the night. From her window she could see the lights of Seattle. What would she see at the island? Stars and empty space? Mom had said it was mostly trees with some shore.

Maybe I should pray something will happen so I don't have to go. But Pam hadn't prayed since Dad's accident. God hadn't listened to her then and saved Dad, so why should He listen to her now? Instead she'd close her eyes and wish real hard. When she woke in the morning, maybe it would all be a bad dream.

Pam huddled into a ball on her bed. There was another reason she didn't want to go—more important than missing all the summer fun, or leaving Seattle, or even Eric Brent. It was the secret she couldn't even tell Mom. When she had promised Dad that she would take care of Mom, she hadn't really known how. Then it had come to her, that wonderful chance to keep her promise! *Seventeen* magazine held an annual short-story contest for teenage writers, *with a big bucks prize!* Even more important, if she won the contest, the editors would probably buy more stories from her. She could also send stories to *Scholastic, Scope,* and *Teen.* Maybe she could even become so famous Mom wouldn't have to teach anymore.

Pam found herself lost in a world of spies. She never knew when her tense body straightened out in sleep. All night long, dark figures along shadowy streets followed her. And Eric Brent popped in and out of her dreams. "I'll call you . . . call you . . . call you."

Was that Eric calling? No, Mom was shaking her. "Time to get up, Pam. We have to get an early start."

Pam slowly climbed out of bed, showered, and dressed. Her heart felt like one big rock. None of her wishing had changed anything. It was morning, bright and beautiful, and Sandwich Island was still waiting for her. She looked at the silent phone, wishing it would ring. But in spite of her slowness, time rushed by.

As she and Mom pulled out of the driveway, Pam looked back—just once. Never had home looked so good. Never had the view from their hill been more beautiful. Never had the Olympic Mountains, across Puget Sound, been so easily seen. She blinked hard to keep from crying and tried to swallow the lump in her throat.

If only they weren't going. If only she could stay and finish her contest story, and really take care of Mom. If only Eric had called. If only, . . . but Pam was too tired to think. She was too numb even to care. Her only consolation was the thought of getting to Sandwich Island. The first thing she would do when she got there was write a note to Eric. It was all she had to look forward to.

Chapter Two

The first thing Pam did at Sandwich Island was to embarrass herself in front of the entire staff!

Pam hadn't expected camp to be anything like it was. Rows of little brown cabins with built-in bunk beds for the boys and their counselors. Grassy open areas with play equipment for the younger boys. Trees and sky and water. If Pam hadn't been so full of misery over leaving Seattle and all her friends and plans, the place might have interested her. As it was, she couldn't even pretend enthusiasm.

"Where do we stay?"

Mom ignored the droop of Pam's lips. "Right over here." She led the way to a small trailer parked back a little way from the cabins. It didn't look very big, but it did have flower beds around it, and it was close to the shower and rest rooms. Pam was so busy looking at it that she ran right into a boy coming up the stairs to the dining hall. Crash!

"Whoa, there!" The boy caught Pam before she fell.

She heard laughter from the staff, who were just going in for a meeting. It made her so angry she snapped, "Why don't you look where you're going?"

"Me!" The red-haired boy had a temper to match. "Maybe you'd better take a good look at yourself!" It didn't help that Pam knew he was right. They stood there glaring at each other until Mom came up. She hadn't seen what happened.

"Oh, Pam, Dennis, I see you've met." This was the boy who was supposed to show her around? Well, Pam wouldn't have to worry about *that* any longer. He disliked her as much as she did him. But Pam was wrong. Dennis's temper cooled as soon as it had flared. He grinned at her.

"Sorry, Pam. Can I help you get settled?" She looked at him suspiciously, then decided to be friendly. He seemed to be the only person anywhere near her age.

"Uh, sure, we have some things to put away." Pam found herself walking to the trailer with the stocky, red-haired boy. Now that she had a good look at him, Pam liked what she saw. The red hair was crisp and curly, his brown eyes were friendly. Besides, he knew his way around. He'd been coming to camp with his parents for the past three years.

"We get boys from 5 to 11 years old. There are usually about 60 at one time. They come and go. Some stay all summer; others for just a week or so."

"All summer? Some of these little kids stay all

summer?" Pam could hardly believe her ears. But Dennis was serious.

"A lot of them don't have any other place to go, Pam." Dennis pointed to a small drooping boy standing all alone by the flower beds. "His parents died a long time ago. He's been living with his aunt and uncle, but the aunt broke her leg. The uncle is old and can't care for them both, so they sent Peter to camp. He'll be here all summer. It's really sad. Peter doesn't act like he misses his aunt and uncle, but he doesn't talk so it's hard to tell."

Pam stared first at Dennis, then at the little forlorn-looking boy by the flower beds. "Doesn't talk? You mean he can't talk?"

Dennis shook his head. "Peter can talk. I've known him since he was born. Until his folks died he was the cutest, smartest little guy you'd ever know. Since then, he hasn't said one word, and it's been almost two years. I've tried and tried, but I can't get him to talk. Neither can anyone else. He won't even be able to go to school, and he's almost 6."

Something in Dennis's voice made Pam stop and stare at him. He really cared about Peter. It showed when he spoke of him. Pam looked at the dark-haired little boy again. She knew how it felt to lose someone. She knew the pain, the terrible aloneness. But Peter had lost both parents—and when he was only 4 years old! For a moment Pam's mouth felt dry. *Why did God let things like this happen?* But she pushed the thought aside.

"Maybe I can help him. I lost my dad, too."

Her words surprised Dennis as well as Pam, but with a big smile that made Pam feel a whole lot better about Sandwich Island, Dennis called, "Peter, come and meet our newcomer."

The little boy's steps were slow. His eyes were dull and lifeless, uninterested. He didn't smile when Pam said, "Hello, Peter."

Peter's hands were still in hers, but he made no response. Yet Pam knew he had heard and understood. Without stopping to think why, Pam dropped to her knees and hugged him. "I hope you'll be my friend, Peter. I didn't want to come here. I don't know any of the boys, and I'm really lonely." For just a moment the dark eyes sparkled. Even Dennis saw it. Shyly Peter squeezed Pam's hand, but just then the dinner bell rang. Without another look at her, Peter turned away and slowly walked to his cabin. Again he was the same drooping little boy Pam had first seen. Dennis just stared after him.

"Do you know that's the most excitement he's shown in the week he's been here? How did you do it?" Dennis looked at Pam even more closely. "Are you really lonely, or did you just say it for Peter?"

Suddenly Pam's feelings broke loose. She told Dennis how her whole summer had been planned and how Mom's job had ruined everything. She told him how she hadn't wanted to come, and how she'd almost prayed to stay home. "But I don't pray anymore." Pam caught the quick glance Dennis gave her, and rushed on. She told him about wanting to win the contest. She told him everything except her promise to Dad—and about Eric Brent. She even told Dennis what Mrs. Johnstone had written on her story outline.

"She's only one person, but how can I finish my spy story up here? I want to win that contest more than anything else in the world! But I won't even have a chance now."

Dennis shook his head. "Well, Pam, I can't dig up any spies, but . . ." he checked the door to see that no one was listening, "we have a mystery right here in camp!"

Pam's eyes glowed. "You do? A real mystery?"

"We sure do. Someone has been taking food from the kitchen storeroom at night. We have checked all the cabins. The counselors say all the boys are in at night. But the food keeps disappearing."

Pam felt some of her disappointment slide away. Disappearing food? Who could be taking it?

Dennis went on. "Just last night some things were taken, but we don't know how! Every single boy was in his cabin. We're too far from town for anyone else to be coming out here at night. There's your mystery, Pam. You can call it the 'Sandwich Summer Camp Mystery' or something!" Before she could ask any more questions, Dennis checked his watch.

"Whoops! I have to get my boys to the dining hall. See you at dinner." But when Dennis was gone, Pam slowly took her contest entry from her suitcase and reread it. Just as she had feared, she couldn't get back into it, not up here. Sandwich Island seemed far removed from dark streets and spies. Maybe Mrs. Johnstone was right. Maybe she should write about things she knew.

With a quick movement, Pam stuffed the contest entry in the bottom of the suitcase and snatched up her pen and notebook. If there was a mystery on the campground, she was going to be in the middle of it! She would take notes, then make her story from them.

Pam had made Mom promise she could eat back in the kitchen the first night. She just couldn't face all those unknown boys. When she heard singing at the tables, a little thrill went through her. Maybe, just maybe, things weren't going to be so bad after all. Dennis seemed nice, and he was at least near her own age. Then there was the mystery.

"Hey, Pam, want to help with devotions at campfire tonight?"

Pam shook her head, her face turning red. "Uh, no, I'll just watch." Devotions! The last thing Pam wanted. But she was curious enough to drift down after the others to see what took place. She had always liked campfires, and Dennis was good with the boys. Their skits were original and lively, and many of the boys participated. They sang a lot, too. Pam was just beginning to relax when Dennis told another story and followed it with a prayer. It wasn't any big deal, and yet Pam felt funny, out of place.

Did the boys really like that kind of stuff, or were they just polite because they liked Dennis? Pam slipped away to the trailer before campfire was quite over. On the way she passed the tiny chapel. She'd been curious about it, such a little building, only about 10 feet square. She'd asked Mom about it. "It's there for anyone who wants to use it, a private place to meditate or just think."

Pam hadn't said anything more about it, but she'd wondered. Who would want to go into that funny little building? Did some of the counselors go there? She supposed they did. Did Dennis ever . . . but she couldn't ask him. It wasn't the kind of thing you asked someone else, especially not someone you'd only met.

Dennis, what a funny kid he was! So stocky, and with a temper, but when he looked at Peter, he was sort of soft. He sure was different from Eric. Pam laughed at the thought. Eric was dark and aloof. Dennis was rumpled and grinning all the time, even in the short time she'd known him.

It wasn't until she had yawned her way through brushing her teeth and was in bed that Pam remembered she'd been going to write a note to Eric. Oh well, she'd do it tomorrow, she was too sleepy now.

Strangely enough, it wasn't Eric's handsome face she saw last before dropping off to sleep. It wasn't even Dennis, or Mom, or Dad, as sometimes she remembered him. It was the small, sad face of the little boy who didn't talk—Peter Piper. Why did such terrible things have to happen? Suddenly all Pam's own problems seemed to grow smaller. If only she could help Peter, the summer wouldn't be entirely wasted. Dad would be proud of her, if he knew. She remembered the feel of the scrawny body in her arms when she'd hugged Peter. There *had* been a sparkle in his eyes.

Chapter Three

Ta-*ta*-ta-ta-ta! Ta-*ta*-ta-ta-ta! Ta-*ta*-ta-ta-ta-ta-*ta*-*ta*!

Pam sat straight up in bed. "What on earth is that?" The hands of the travel alarm pointed to 6 o'clock. Where was she? This wasn't her room at home. And 6 o'clock! She couldn't remember ever being up at this time of day. Her sleep-filled eyes roved the room, noticing the empty bed. Oh, yes. Mom was already up. They were at boys' camp, and that must have been the getting-up bugle. What did they call it? Reveille, yes. How disgusting! Mom had to be up at 5 to help start breakfast.

With a grunt, Pam dropped back on the pillow. No reason for *her* to get up. Breakfast wasn't until 7. She was almost back to sleep when she heard someone at the door. The noise wasn't loud. It was more like someone scratching.

Reaching for a robe, Pam went to the door, barefooted.

"*Good* morning!" Dennis Kincaid's grin was the last straw. "Did you sleep well?"

Pam glared at him. "What are you doing up in the middle of the night?" She sounded cross, even to herself.

Dennis didn't seem to notice. "Middle of the night! It's the best part of the day. Look!" He waved an arm toward the bay and the sky, colored by the rising sun. "Smell the salt air. Listen to the birds. How can you sleep when all this beautiful summer is going to waste out here?" He pulled Peter Piper from behind him to face Pam. "We came to ask you to have breakfast with us." Peter just stared, but Pam thought she saw a little flicker of interest in his dark eyes. It was enough.

"I'll be ready in a few minutes." After all, why not get up? She would have had to in a few more minutes, anyway. It was nice of Dennis to stop by for her. He couldn't know how she had dreaded going all alone the first time into that dining hall full of boys. The Kincaids had told her it was all right, she'd get to know them, but the first time would be hard.

If Pam had known what Dennis Kincaid was up to, she'd have crawled back into bed and pulled the covers over her head! They were among the first in the line, so they got to their table ahead of the others. That was fine with Pam. Now she could eat her breakfast in peace, then get acquainted later. That was what she thought! Instead, when all the boys were served and the blessing had been asked, Dennis stood up.

"I have an announcement. We have a newcomer. Her name's Pam. She'll be here all summer."

For one awful moment 60 pairs of boys' eyes stared at her. Then 60 pairs of boys' eyes sparkled, and 60 boys' voices chorused, "Hi, Pam!"

She managed to get out a weak "Hi" before turning on Dennis. "How could you? I've never been so embarrassed in my whole life!"

Dennis's eyes opened wide. "Not even when you ran into me on the steps yesterday?"

Pam could feel hot flags of color in her face. She ducked her head and didn't answer. Then she caught sight of Peter. He was looking at her anxiously, with a strained expression. Was it the anger in her voice that had brought fear to his eyes? Pam changed her scolding to a laugh and told him, "Anyway, I have my friend here with me!"

Peter's skinny hand slipped into Pam's as if to reassure her. Never had Pam been so thrilled. She had always wanted a little brother or sister and never had one. Peter was responding! Dennis saw it too, but kept still. His eyes, across Peter's head, seemed to warn Pam not to push. Peter had to do it himself. Pam nodded, understanding, and squeezed Peter's hand, then went back to eating. But her mind was going in circles. She still didn't like being away from Seattle, yet there hadn't been any dull moments since she had arrived at camp, that was for sure!

When breakfast was over, Dennis and Peter went with the others, leaving Pam to herself. She felt she was in a funny position. She wasn't on the staff, but she wasn't really part of the camp, either. She shrugged her shoulders, wondering what she could do, and finally decided to look around.

"I'm going to take a walk,"

Mom looked up from her work, too busy to do more than smile and say, "Have fun, dear."

Pam was really surprised to see how big the camp was! Dennis had told her it was an 80-acre piece of ground. He'd also told her something of the history of how it had become a church camp.

"A wonderful couple, Norwegian people, bought the land many years ago. They didn't even know why they bought it!"

Pam had stared at him. "Then why *did* they buy it?"

Dennis looked her square in the eye. "They felt the Lord wanted them to." At Pam's disbelieving look he went on with his story. He didn't want to argue with her. "Anyway, they felt strongly they should buy it, although the man had always wanted a big farm, and this land was too stony for farming. I don't know how much they paid. It wouldn't seem like much now, but it was a lot of money in those days. Years passed and then our church found we were going to have to move from our other camp. There was overcrowding, and the Health Department was about to close it—something to do with sanitation. I guess the church leaders didn't know what to do.

They'd always had a wonderful camp. Now there was no place to hold it."

Dennis stopped but Pam was too eager to wait until he caught his breath. "What happened?"

Dennis's face was serious. "The Norwegian couple *gave* this property to the church."

Pam gasped. "They *gave* it away? Eighty acres?"

"Yes. They said that after all those years of just having the land, not knowing what to do with it, they now knew why they'd felt they should buy it in the first place."

"I can't believe it."

"It's true, Pam. My folks were in on the whole thing." Dennis had laughed. "I remember as a little kid coming up for work parties. Everything you see was built with volunteer labor—the dining hall, the rest rooms, the cabins, everything. We lived in tents, and the women cooked in the old farmhouse. Was it ever neat!"

Now as Pam slowly walked around the grounds she found herself thinking of the story. She remembered how Dennis had told her how the people had shared. Sometimes it rained hard, and the tents leaked. But people still came and worked. For a minute she closed her eyes, seeing all the tents in the big cleared space in the middle of the trees, seeing pouring rain, seeing people who were wet but smiling. A strange loneliness went through her.

"I wish I could have been here." Pam hadn't realized she'd spoken out loud until a small brown rabbit by the path hopped a little and stood waiting for her to go by.

Pam's tour was complete. She walked from one end of the camp to the other. Dennis' comments came back to her. When she went to the big barn that had been converted into a rustic church used for worship services, she thought of what he had told her.

"We used to get fined a nickel if we called it a barn. We had to call it a church, even from the very first." It was dim and quiet inside, shadowy after being outside in the sunlight. Someone had banked greens in front of the speaker's stand.

The church was so quiet and peaceful that Pam dropped down onto one of the big old-fashioned folding benches. She could hear birds singing and noticed some had built their nests just under the eaves inside the building. The thought crossed her mind, *They probably feel safe here, living inside a church!* Again that strange pang of loneliness filled her. If only she could feel safe—if only Dad could be here! For the first time since Dad had died, Pam broke down, sobbing out some of her bitterness. How Dad would have loved all this! He'd always said that when he retired they might be able to help with camps, like the Kincaids. Now it wouldn't come true.

A rustling behind her caused Pam to whirl around. "Who's there?"

"Sorry, Pam." A red-faced Dennis came to the shadowy corner where she was huddled. "Is there anything I can do to help?"

"There's nothing anyone can do! No one can bring my dad back to life, and that's what I need!" Dennis stayed quiet for a long moment. "Pam, was your dad saved?"

"Saved? You mean a Christian? Sure. We've gone to church as far back as I can remember."

Dennis's face was serious. "That's not what I mean. I mean, did he know the Lord Jesus Christ?" He hesitated, then, "Do you?"

Pam's chin went up in the air. "Of course. Everyone knows about God and Jesus."

Dennis was patient. "That's still not what I mean. Everyone does know *about* God and Jesus, but it's not the same thing as knowing personally the Lord Jesus Christ and our heavenly Father." He saw Pam's confusion. "It's like—like—everyone knows *about* the president of the United States. But how many people have opened their hearts and homes to him, asked him to come in and live with them, to rule their lives?"

Pam was still. When she spoke, it was slowly. "I see what you mean, but I don't see why I'm not saved. I've gone to church since I was a baby, and—"

"Don't you see?" Dennis leaned forward in his earnestness. "It isn't enough. That was your parents' choice for you. You have to make your own commitment." He looked straight at her. "The Bible says, 'Believe in the Lord Jesus, and you will be saved.'* Do you really believe, Pam?"

"How can I?" There was despair in her cry. "If

God is the kind and loving God He's supposed to be, why did He let Dad die?"

"When we believe on Jesus and personally accept Him into our lives, we'll never die."

"Oh, heaven. Sure, I know about that. But I need Dad now!"

Dennis looked at her in pity. "Pam, what you *really* need is to know that the Lord Jesus Christ is with you all the time."

"How can He be?" She was trying hard to grasp it. "He died. He isn't here."

"But He promised to send His Holy Spirit to us, to guide us."

"Is that why you're so happy all the time?"

"It's why I know I am loved all the time. God didn't promise that we'd be happy all the time. He just promised that through His Son we'd be forgiven and be able to learn to live with Him forever."

Pam sighed. "I wish I could believe that."

"You can, Pam." But she jumped up, torn between what Dennis was saying and her own loss. Dennis sensed she needed time to consider what he had told her. In his heart a prayer went up for Pam, that she might find the only way that would ever bring her joy. "Want to walk down to the lake?"

"Lake?" Some of Pam's confusion was lost in her surprise. "I didn't know there was a lake."

"Sure." Dennis led the way. "It's controlled by tides, a salt-water lake." Before they got near it, Peter Piper came running. "Want a canoe ride?"

"Is it all right? I wouldn't want to get in trouble or anything."

"The camp director said you could do whatever you wanted." Dennis helped Peter and Pam into life jackets. "This is rule number one. Nobody goes out without a life jacket." He picked up a paddle. "First a canoe trip, then Peter and I can show you the woods later. OK, old man?" Peter still didn't smile, but he did scrunch down closer to Pam.

"I wish Wendy could be here." Pam looked around, then added, "On the other hand, she probably wouldn't fit in." She thought of Eric. "My friends back home are really city people. They might not like all this." She didn't notice how Peter look at her, then how his dark eyes traveled from shore to bay and back to her.

"You like it, don't you?"

Pam didn't feel the way Peter tensed up, or how he relaxed when she exclaimed, "I love it! I didn't want to come, but I didn't know how beautiful it would be!" She suddenly remembered Peter and smiled at him. "Then, too, I have my new friend." She was glad for the answering sparkle in his eyes.

"Two new friends." Dennis sounded gruff as he swung the canoe toward shore. "And the best friend of all—if you'll only let Him be." Pam's eyes met his. *Why, he really cares whether I accept the Lord!* But she wasn't ready to commit herself. God hadn't kept her dad from dying. Could she really trust Him with her whole life? Somehow, from what Dennis said, she knew that's what accepting His Son would be—a forever kind of promise. She wasn't ready for that.

"I wish you weren't so busy. It's going to be lonely by myself."

"Why don't you help? I've been here for three years. Campers are 5 to 11, so when I turned 12 I couldn't come as a camper anymore. Our director's neat—he made me a special helper that year, then a junior counselor. There must be something you can do." He laughed. "I was a real gopher, at first, you know—'Dennis, go-fer this, Dennis, go-fer that!'"

Pam couldn't help but join his laughter. Dennis was no dummy, even if he weren't Eric. "You really love it here, don't you?"

"Yes, I do." Dennis led Peter away to wash up for supper.

As Pam watched them go, sudden determination filled her. If Dennis liked it that much, then she'd be a good sport this summer. She'd ask the camp director for something to do and come up with a story that would win the contest. If it were too late for this time, there was always another year! *Dennis said write a story and call it the "Sandwich Summer Camp Mystery" or something. Well, first I have to solve the mystery. I'll snoop around and put Nancy Drew out of business!* She raced up the trail. She could spend a half-hour watching before supper-time. She found a big tree a little way from the door to the food storeroom. But no one came in or out, not even the cooks. She'd just have to spy at night. Dennis said that's when the food disappeared.

Pam could feel her excitement growing. What a great story, based on a real mystery! Mrs. Johnstone had told her to write about what she knew. What better way to do that than to catch the thief and then write it into her contest entry? Gone was her promise to herself to write to Eric.

Dennis commented at supper, "Who handed you a million dollars?"

"You did." Pam laughed at his expression. "You told me there was a mystery." She glanced at Peter's round eyes and listening ears. "My teacher said to write what I know, so—" She left the sentence dangling, but when Peter took his tray away, she whispered, "Instead of writing about spies, I'm going to become one!"

That night the memory of Dennis' serious face bothered Pam. She finally asked, "Mom, was Dad saved?"

There was a long silence. Was Mom asleep? Then a low voice replied, "Yes, Pam, he was. He accepted the Lord when he was a child."

For a moment Pam felt warmth rise in her, relief. Then Dad was all right, he was saved! But—"Mom, are you?"

"No, Pam." Again all was still. "Your father and I came from different churches. My church doesn't call it being saved. It's enough just to believe in God and Jesus and do good." She sighed. "But since I've been up here and seen all these people—I wonder. I wish we'd gone to your dad's church, instead of mine. I don't think just believing is enough. The

Kincaids, the camp director, even the youngsters have a living something I don't have. It's as though God is walking with them all the time. I want to learn more. I'd like to have that personal relationship with God that the Kincaids have."

But long after Mom was asleep, Pam lay awake thinking.

---

*The *Holy Bible, New International Version.* Copyright © 1973, 1978, International Bible Society. Used by permission of Zondervan Bible Publishers.

Chapter Four

Pam looked across the desk at the camp director. "Mr. Grayson, I need something to do."

Mr. Grayson met her blue eyes squarely. He had wondered how she would fit in, an almost-13-year-old girl in the middle of his boys' camp! Now as he saw her earnest face he relaxed. She'd be fine, just fine.

"I'd like to volunteer to help with camp. But I don't know what I can do. I've only been here a little while. I don't really feel part of camp, but I want to." Her last words were almost a whisper. Mr. Grayson sat silently for a few minutes, then smiled at Pam. What he said was the last thing in the world she might have expected!

"Your mother tells me you like to read and want to be a writer." Pam felt her face turning red. Why had Mom told him that? She dropped her eyes to her hands, tightly squeezed together now in her lap.

Her writing ambitions were private, not just to be thrown out in the open for everyone to discuss. But Mr. Grayson wasn't through. "There *is* something you could do, Pam, something to really help."

She could feel the sincerity in Mr. Grayson's voice, and it took away her embarrassment. She looked at him and leaned forward.

"For a long time we've needed someone to be with the younger boys during staff meeting. Those boys from about 7 or 8 on up know what the 'honor system' is and pretty much take care of themselves. But the 5- and 6-year-olds need someone to be with them. That's the time of day they get homesick—if they get homesick at all. The rest of the time they're too busy.

"Dennis has been trying to help by telling them stories, but he misses staff meetings, and besides, he's better in sports than as a storyteller. How would you like to give it a try, Pam? It would be from 4 o'clock to 5 o'clock every day. You can use whatever stories you wish." Mr. Grayson grinned at her. "Maybe you'll even want to write some of your own!"

For just a minute Pam was lost in a daydream of writing stories for the boys, then later putting them in a collection. A children's book! That's what she could do! That would be even better than winning the *Seventeen* contest. It would bring in a lot more money. She could keep her promise to Dad. Maybe Mom wouldn't even have to go back to work next year.

"How about it, Pam?"

"I'd love to!" She stopped for a second. "But where do I get the books?"

The camp director waved to a shelf behind him. "There are some here. You're welcome to whatever you can find. But Pam, if you could *tell* the stories instead of read them—you know, stories like *The Little Red Hen* or *The Little Engine That Could* or other stories you liked when you were 5 and 6—it would be a lot better. You'll only have about a half-dozen boys. But it would really help us out. I was serious about your writing some of your own, too. Where could you find a better place to try them out than right here?"

"When do I start?" Pam could feel her heart pumping.

Mr. Grayson looked at her and laughed. "I can announce it at lunch. No reason you can't start today, is there?"

Pam gasped but her chin went up. "That's fine with me."

She didn't catch Mr. Grayson's look of approval. Instead she ran to the kitchen to tell her mother. The kitchen was dark, so she went on to their trailer. "Mom, I have a job!"

Mrs. Jones had finished her morning chores and was in the trailer resting before the noonday preparations. She couldn't tell Pam how strenuous her job was. It would only upset her. She had worried about Pam's reaction to coming to Sandwich Island.

41

Now the happiness in her daughter's face did a lot to relieve her.

Pam was glowing. "I'm going to tell stories to the little boys every day for an hour. Mr. Grayson says during staff meeting when all the grownups are in the dining hall some of the younger boys get homesick. It's the only time they have free. They're too busy the rest of the day, and too tired at night to stay awake! He says I can really be a big help, and I can even write my own stories!"

"That's wonderful, Pam. You really *can* be a help. The Kincaids were mentioning just this morning how much we need someone to take care of the little ones during staff meetings. We can't; we're too busy getting supper. You'll be perfect."

Mom's approval made Pam's day. She rushed to her mother and hugged her. "You know, I didn't believe there would be *any*thing neat up here, but there really is!"

Mom's eyes shone but she only said, "Which story are you going to tell first?"

Pam's lower lip stuck out as she thought hard. "I'm going to start with *The Little Engine That Could.*" She got up and marched around the tiny trailer. "You know, 'I *think* I can, I *think* I can,'" she puffed like a train.

Mom couldn't help but laugh. "Those kids will love it. What others are you going to use? You know, stories go faster than you think, and you have a whole hour."

"I always liked the one about the cats. 'Hundreds

of cats, thousands of cats, millions and billions and trillions of cats!'" She chanted it as she had when she had been 6. For a moment the happiness faded, the bright color left her face. Dad had done that one with her. But she refused to think of it. Mom saw the struggle in Pam's face and sensed what caused it. Almost she reached out, but before she could move a loud voice came from outside.

"Swimming time!" Dennis and his shadow Peter were at the door. Pam knew Dennis was the lifeguard for the little kids. It would be a good time for her to go swimming. She could also watch the 5- and 6-year-olds and see if the stories she had planned would be for their age.

Pam could hardly wait to tell Dennis her big news as they rounded up the other little boys and led them down to the lake. Everyone except Peter had gone into the water in the shallow lake. They took care to stay at the near end, since the lake quickly got deeper. Pam couldn't wait any longer. Besides, it would be nice for Peter to have a secret.

Pam made her voice as mysterious as she could. "Peter, Dennis, can you keep a secret until after lunch?"

"Sure." Dennis looked surprised. "We can keep a secret, can't we, old man?" Peter's eyes got big, and he inched closer to Pam. His head nodded just a little. *If only he would say something*, Pam thought, but she smiled at the solemn boy by her knee.

"I'm going to tell stories to the little boys every day during staff meeting!" This time there was no mistaking the look in Peter's eyes. He really lit up! He squeezed her hand in his grimy one. For a minute Pam even thought he was going to smile.

"Run along into the water, Peter," Dennis told him. "I'll wait for Pam to kick off her shoes." Reluctantly the little boy moved away. When Peter was out of hearing distance, Dennis took Pam's hand and squeezed it the same way Peter had done. "Pam, if you don't do anything else this whole summer, the way you've started to get through to Peter is worth your being here."

Funny the way Pam's heart leaped. She hadn't known how much she wanted Dennis' approval. At that moment, if someone had asked her about Eric, she would probably have said, "Eric who?"

It was a special moment, broken when one of the boys, sitting on a low diving board, called out to Dennis. "Look at me, Dennis!" The boy was holding his nose, ready to jump.

"Wait a minute, there!" Dennis was gone in a flash, keeping watch over his boys like a mother hen with her chicks. But Pam didn't forget the way his eyes had shone when he found out she was going to tell stories. She didn't forget the way he'd squeezed her hand and smiled at her.

Why did the stocky, redhead boy suddenly seem so neat? Pam didn't have time to think of it just then because Dennis hollered, "Come on, Pam, we'll teach these kids to swim."

The next hour was a splashy good time as the boys learned to kick and even paddle a bit. Dennis helped the more advanced; Pam worked with the real beginners. She had only Peter and one other boy, and by the end of the hour the second boy had graduated to Dennis' group.

"Like this, Peter," Pam told him, swallowing hard at the sight of how thin he was in his swim trunks. Once more the thought crossed her mind, *Why, God?* But the next instant she had completely forgotten it in watching Peter's face light up as he managed to struggle a foot or two without her help.

As Pam showered and washed the salt water from her hair before the noon meal, she found herself whistling, the first time in ages.

I wonder why I'm so happy? Why do I feel so content? Is it because I'm helping others? It was a big thought to have in a camp shower, too big. Besides, she had to dash for the trailer and get her hair partly dry before the meal. It sure was easy to get hungry up here. She was starved all the time!

"I can see it all now," Pam was talking to herself through the big towel over her head. "When I get home, I'll weigh a ton. But who cares? I've always been too skinny, anyway." She flipped her hair out, ran a comb through it, and headed for the dining hall. Dennis and Peter would be saving her a place. And Mr. Grayson would be making the announcement about the story hour. She could hardly wait!

When the meal was over Mr. Grayson stood up. "We have a special activity for the 5- and 6-year-olds. Our new girl, Pam, will lead out in a story hour today during staff meeting!" The boys cheered, but

Peter reached over and squeezed Pam's hand. He opened his mouth, and for a minute Pam thought he was going to speak. He didn't, but he nodded his head up and down, telling her *he* had already known about the story hour, it was *their* secret. When they went out of the dining hall, Pam gave him a big hug, and this time, for the very first time, he even hugged her back, just a little, then ran off as if afraid of what he'd done.

Pam asked Dennis, "Is he afraid to like people?"

Dennis said, "We think because he lost his parents he's afraid to like people for fear something will make them go away. When you're 4 years old, you don't understand about death."

Before Pam thought, she blurted out, "You don't understand it when you're almost 13, either." She couldn't face the pity in Dennis' face and turned from him, running away almost the same way Peter had done. When she got to the trailer, she thought how she must have looked to Dennis, a great big girl running off to her trailer to hide.

One of the hardest things Pam ever had to do was force herself to step back down from the trailer and return to where Dennis was. "Sorry, Dennis. Sometimes things get to be too much."

"Do you want to talk about it?"

"Yes." Suddenly Pam did. Dennis led her to the little chapel she had seen earlier, letting her go in first. It was so small! And quiet. There were just two benches, a picture of Christ in front, and candles, and a vase of fresh flowers. But it was peaceful, the perfect place for their talk.

"What was your dad like?"

Pam's face lighted up. "Really great." She sighed and added, "Dennis, I asked Mom last night. Dad was saved, really saved. He accepted Jesus when he was just a little boy."

"Then why haven't you—" Dennis' face turned beet red.

"It's all right." Pam tried to find words to explain. "Dad and Mom were from different churches. I guess they were waiting until I was old enough to choose for myself. But I think Mom regrets it now." She repeated what her mother had said. "Maybe if Mom accepts the Lord, I will, too."

"No, Pam, no!" Dennis' protest shocked her. His face was stern. "You can't wait for anyone else, not even your mom, not when it comes to knowing the Lord and accepting Him. Only *you* can do that. It doesn't matter if your parents are the finest people on earth and the best Christians. You've got to accept the Lord Jesus as your own personal Saviour and be born again in order to be saved."

"I don't know Him that well. How can I be sure He won't let me down?"

Dennis sighed. "Before you came up here, did you personally examine every nut and bolt and screw in your car? Did you think 'I'd better not try it; it might not get me there'? Of course not! That's where faith comes in, Pam. We have to repent of our sins and believe God's Word."

"I'm not such a great sinner."

"The greatest sin is not accepting the Lord and rebelling against Him. Can you honestly say you've never done that?"

Pam was silent, remembering how she'd poured out her bitterness, her resentment, that Dad had been taken.

"Pam, a long time ago my family moved all the time—from one place to the next. I used to ask God Why? Every time I made new friends, we'd move. I got so I didn't like God very much."

"You?" Pam couldn't believe it.

"Yes, me. I figured if God cared anything about me, He'd let me stay with my friends. I'd accepted Him when I was small, but it didn't make it any easier. I finally figured out that the same God who allowed me to move away from my friends helped me make new ones."

What a funny thing to say! Pam stared at him, but Dennis wasn't through. "Maybe it's the same with you, Pam. If your dad had lived, would you be here now? If not, who would have helped Peter?"

Pam jumped up, eyes blazing. "You're crazy! You're trying to tell me God let Dad die so I could come up here and meet Peter?"

Dennis was patient. "That's not what I said, Pam. Listen, will you?"

Pam sat down again, but there was distrust in her eyes.

"We aren't going to know all the 'whys' in this life. And we don't have to like it, but that's how it is." Dennis scratched his head as he tried to explain. "I don't know why God didn't make a miracle and let your dad live. But He didn't. You can blame Him, but it won't change things. Your dad was ready to go. What if he hadn't been?" He let it sink in.

"I don't even pretend to know why your dad died. But since it happened, God still can make good out of it. Do you think it was just chance your mom was asked to come up here, and that you came, too? No way."

"Then I'm nothing but a puppet." Pam's voice was bitter. "God dangles the strings and I jump. Is that it?"

"You're no puppet, Pam. You have your own choices to make. You could have ignored Peter. But you hugged him—and look what happened." Pam didn't answer and Dennis stood up. "I'm not trying to preach, Pam, but you can't run away from God. What's past is past. What counts is what you do *now.*" The door closed quietly behind him as he left Pam alone with her thoughts.

What if Dennis was right? What if it was all part of a plan, her coming here with Mom? She thought of the wistfulness in her mom's voice—*I wonder— something I don't have.* Was Jesus the answer? For both Mom and her?

Chapter Five

Pam felt a thrill when she led her little group of boys down the path to the amphitheater. The minute the bell rang at 4 o'clock, they had appeared like magic, waiting for her by the door of the trailer. After her talk with Dennis, Pam had gone back and thrown herself on her bed, tired from trying to figure things out. Surprisingly, she had fallen asleep. When the bell rang, it took her a minute to know where she was.

Then Pam remembered. "My story hour!" She grabbed a comb and ran it through her hair, then stepped outside. The first thing she noticed was that Peter was in front of the others, evidently waiting for her. There was no question as he took his place at the head of her line, right by her side. Pam felt a strange little tug at the hem of her shirt and saw that Peter was hanging on, shyly, just enough to be touching her. She smiled and announced, "Hey, this is going to be great! Where shall we go?"

"The campfire place." The little boys scrambled around her, faces eager. No homesickness in them now! Again Pam felt a warm glow. It was nice to be needed.

It didn't take long for the group to reach the log benches that had been built into an amphitheater. But instead of sitting on the logs, they all sat in a circle on blankets Pam had brought. Peter made sure he was right next to Pam, sitting cross-legged like the others, but close enough to lean against her. None of the other boys seemed to mind. They crowded close and waited. Pam looked into their upturned faces, such small, anxious boys!

"We're going to do *The Little Engine That Could.*" As blue eyes, brown eyes, and green eyes watched her, Pam told the story to them. When it was over, she jumped up and led them through all the motions. The boys were excited.

"I *think* I can, I *think* I can!" The line marched faster. But when Pam started, "I *knew* I could, I *knew* I could!" the whole line broke into a run, finally collapsing in laughter on the blankets. It took them a little while to get their breath, and when they did Pam told them her old favorite story about all the cats. When she came to the part, "Hundreds of cats, thousands of cats, millions and billions and trillions of cats," they joined in. Although Pam didn't know it, those first two stories would be the boys' special stories. Every day for as long as she was there they would ask for them—along with another story—one she hadn't planned on!

"Tell us another story, Pam, tell us another!" If the boys' cries were to be believed, Pam's first story hour was a huge success. The six little boys couldn't get enough stories.

Pam looked at her watch. She couldn't believe it. She still had 20 minutes? She shook her watch and held it to her ear, but its steady ticking showed her it hadn't stopped. What could she do? She had used all the stories she had prepared for today. She opened her mouth to tell them that was all, but the looks on their faces, all waiting for another story, stopped her.

"How . . . how would you like a story I can make up?"

"Yes, yes!" The boys clapped and scooted even closer, Peter pressing against Pam's knee. Pam dropped her voice to a low, spooky note and began.

"Once upon a time there was a summer camp for boys, just like your camp." The boys looked at each other, their eyes big and wide. They were going to like this story!

Pam went on, keeping her voice mysterious. "Everyone had a good time at camp. There were all kinds of things to do. Swimming and hiking and lots of good food. There even was a story hour!" This time the boys laughed right out. But Pam continued, "There was only one thing wrong in the whole camp—there was a mystery!" She leaned forward and the boys scooted in even closer. They didn't want to miss one word!

"The cooks were the first to notice it. When they

went to get certain food to fix the meals, the food wasn't there!" One of the boys gasped. "Someone was stealing food at the camp. The cooks asked around. The camp director asked around. But none of the boys knew anything about it. Pretty soon everyone got so worried about it that the boys' camp wasn't happy anymore. No one wanted to be at camp with someone who stole. But no one knew what to do. They just didn't know how to catch the food bandit!"

Butch, the biggest boy asked, "What's a bandit?" The question caught Pam unprepared.

"A bandit is a . . . a robber. A thief. Someone who steals. Someone bad. A holdup man." She could see that some of the boys still didn't understand.

"Just a minute!" Pam stepped behind a big tree nearby. In her pocket she had an old black scarf. Quickly she folded it, then tied it around under her eyes and across her nose.

"Wow!" Even Butch shivered when Pam came back. Peter looked at her, then decided it was still Pam. She dropped back to her place on the blanket.

"A bandit wears a mask like this, except he has holes in it for his eyes. Tomorrow I'll cut holes and show you." She took off the black scarf and tucked it into her pocket again. She could hear the sighs of relief. The boys hadn't liked her to wear the mask.

"Anyway, the boys at camp decided they must catch the food bandit. They watched . . . and watched . . . and watched. But they couldn't catch him. At last one of them had a bright idea. When everyone else in camp was asleep, he slipped out of bed and hid behind a big tree, just like the big tree by our kitchen door. For a long time he watched. Pretty soon he got too tired and fell asleep. When he awoke, he heard a creaking noise. The door of the storeroom was opening . . ."

Ding-dong! Ding-dong! The dinner bell rang.

"Our story, our story!" The boys were disappointed.

"I'll tell some more tomorrow," Pam promised, glad for the bell. She had been wondering how she could ever solve the mystery and end the story! It gave her an idea. She'd use it as a continued story until she could come up with a good ending. Now she'd have time to think of something.

"I'll bring the mask tomorrow, too," Pam told the boys as they dashed up the trail to get washed for supper.

But the next day as they all went to the beach, Butch spoke up. Pam had been afraid the boys would demand an end to the story but Butch told her, "We all think you shouldn't tell the rest of the story. Make it last longer. Don't tell the end yet." The boys had been excited. Now this was just what she had hoped for. She'd have extra time to try and come up with a good ending.

If only I could really solve the mystery, the one right here at Sandwich Island. Then I'd have a good ending! But although the food kept disappearing, Pam was no closer to finding out who was taking it than she had been the day she came!

If Pam had known her little shadow Peter was listening a few days later, she would never have talked to Dennis the way she did. Dennis had invited her to take a walk through the uncleared woods during recreation. The counselors took turns working with the boys, so each could have some free time now and then. Dennis and Pam walked a long way up the trail to where a cross had been put in the ground. It was a nice spot. There was moss on the logs, and the sun filtered down through the trees. Pam dropped to a log and relaxed.

"How's your story hour coming?" Dennis sat down across from her.

"Just great, but I have a problem! I don't know how to finish the story. I'm glad these boys are all going to be here awhile yet. None of them know the story is true. Sandwich Island Camp has a food bandit. What am I going to do when it's time to come up with an ending?"

Dennis grinned. "You *are* in a fix! You know, Pam, we've watched and watched but just can't find out who's taking the food. Some more disappeared last night."

Neither of them saw Peter crouched behind the big tree just past them. Their voices carried clearly. He had followed them instead of playing on the swings with the others. He knew he shouldn't be there, but Pam and Dennis were his whole world. Now his ears were wide open, and his eyes bulged out. The story was *true?* There was a food bandit *right here at their own camp?*

"I sure don't know how I'm going to end my story when there isn't any ending," Pam complained. "I sure wish I had some friend who would tell me what to do!"

She laughed and stood up, but Peter ducked back out of sight. Pam needed a friend. Pam had said he was her friend. Could he help her?

Peter slipped back down the trail to camp as fast as his legs would go. He'd surprise Pam, that's what he'd do. He'd find out for her who was taking food. Then she could end her story. No one saw the little smile that curled across his face, the first smile in a long time. No one knew he had heard Dennis and Pam talking.

Peter was very quiet at dinner that night. Pam was the first to notice. He ate as usual, but even though he never talked, there was something different about him.

"Don't you feel good, Peter?"

His dark eyes opened wide. But before he could answer, Mr. Grayson stood up. "It has come to my attention we have two very special people in camp this week. Two people are having birthdays!"

The boys cheered, but Pam felt her face get red. Had Mom told? Mr. Kincaid was bringing in a huge cake on a big cart. He wheeled it right over to where Pam sat. Mr. Grayson said, "Today is Peter Piper's birthday!" All the boys cheered again, but Mr. Grayson's little speech wasn't over. "Pam's birthday actually isn't until tomorrow, but we thought she wouldn't mind sharing a cake with Peter." Pointing to the big letters on the cake, the camp director read aloud, "Happy birthday, Peter and Pam."

Peter's eyes looked as if they would pop from his head, and Pam felt her own must look the same! She had been wondering if anything would be done for her birthday. At home she'd always had a party. For just a moment she remembered other birthdays, when Dad was alive, but Dennis jumped up and hollered, "Speech!"

Somehow Pam got to her feet, with all those boys' eyes on her. It didn't bother her anymore. She grabbed Peter by the hand and had him stand up next to her. Then she said, "Peter and I thank you very much!"

All the boys and the staff sang "Happy Birthday," but Dennis sang the loudest of all. When they were cutting and serving the cake, he whispered, "Now you're a teenager!" Pam just grinned. She had seen the glow in Peter's eyes when they made a wish, then blew out the candles together, every single one of them! Had she ever had a happier birthday? Peter's joy was worth all of it.

Dennis walked Pam to the trailer as the boys spilled out of the dining hall for a good run before campfire. He could hardly wait until they were out of hearing distance to grab Pam's arm.

"Did you see Peter? When they first brought in the cake? Pam, he *smiled*!"

Pam stared at Dennis. "Peter smiled? Are you sure, Dennis?"

"Of course I'm sure. Weren't you watching?"

"No. I was thinking about Dad." Pam swallowed, then looked up at Dennis. "You know, for the first time, it didn't hurt so much."

Dennis wanted to say something, but decided against it. Now wasn't the time. "Good! Anyway, Peter looked at that big cake, and his whole face lit up. He smiled. Then he saw me looking at him, and it faded. Pam, do you realize what you've done for that kid? Just by being his friend?"

But if Dennis and Pam had known how Peter was even then planning to be Pam's friend, they wouldn't have been so happy.

Chapter Six

Pam nibbled the end of her pencil, then started writing.

Dear Wendy,

Sorry I haven't written sooner. You know, I thought I'd hate it here. I really don't. I've never been in a place where so much is going on. By the time the end of the day comes, I'm so sleepy it's all I can do to remember to brush my teeth, let alone write any letters!

The biggest news in camp right now is my story hour. The 5- and 6-year-olds liked it so much that by the end of the week something happened none of us had expected. Four of the 7-year-olds came.

"Can we hear the stories, too?" My boys looked at each other. I think they were torn between wanting to show off how good the stories were and wanting to keep me all for themselves.

Finally Butch told them, "Yeah, you can stay—if

you're quiet." You should have seen him scowl at the bigger boys! They were quiet, all right. They were also so excited about my stories that the next day *all* the 7-year-olds and half the 8-year-olds came! Now I have nearly every boy under 10 in the whole camp—coming each day! It's really a mob, but they love it, so how can I turn them down? At first I thought the 5- and 6-year-olds might not like it, but we solved that by letting them stay right by me on the blankets. The older boys sit in a circle behind them. But Peter is always the closest.

Wendy, I never knew it was possible to love a boy as much as I love Peter. He's so neat, I wish you could meet him! I'm starting to make a real impression on him, too, and I know he likes me or he wouldn't sit so close!

I've decided I may write children's stories for a living. Of all the stories I tell, they like the one I'm making up best. It's about a food bandit who steals food at camp. Every day I add more details and put on a silly mask I made out of my old black scarf. The only thing is—I don't know how to end the story. Some of the boys will be leaving soon, and they will want to know the end. If only we could find out who's taking food here at *our* camp it would help!

Wendy, I'm really worried about Peter. Even though I know I'm making progress, he always looks so tired, as if he isn't sleeping enough! Dennis says Peter is in his cabin and the first one asleep every night. It just doesn't make sense.

Well, I have to get this ready for the mailbox

before the rural-delivery carrier comes. He's really nice and drives a Jeep. Hope you're having a great summer.

Love,
Pam

Pam could hardly keep her eyes open long enough to stamp the letter and run it to the box. The mail carrier came early, so she had to put it out the night before. She was so sleepy she didn't realize she'd forgotten one very important thing in the letter—to tell Wendy how old Peter was—and Dennis! When Wendy got the letter and ran into Eric Brent the next day, she decided to have some fun.

"Hi, Eric! I just got a letter from Pam."

Eric looked puzzled. "Pam?" Wendy was impatient, bursting with her news.

"Sure, Pam Jones. She's up at a boys' camp on Sandwich Island for the summer. Do you want to read her letter? They must really have neat boys up there. She talks about Peter and Dennis, and . . ." The rest of Wendy's sentence was lost as Eric grabbed for the letter. His eyes narrowed as he read the hasty scrawl, then he handed the letter back to Wendy.

"Maybe I'll just run up there," Eric drawled. "But don't tell her I'm coming. I'm getting my brand-new red car tomorrow, and it would be a good spin. You know, go up and take her for a ride, or something."

Wendy swallowed a gasp. Boy, had she ever started something! Wait until Pam saw Eric drive up in his new car. She'd probably forget all about that Peter—but fast!

Pam had intended to stay up nights and watch for the food thief, but between the good cooking and fresh air, she kept putting it off. One night she looked at Mom, already asleep, who looked more rested than she had since Dad died, in spite of her hard work. Once she'd gotten into the swing of cooking, she'd caught on fast. Now she was tan and looked peaceful.

It's been good for both of us. Pam yawned. *Besides, I wouldn't have met Dennis or Peter.* A little smile went over her face. *Funny, I never did get around to writing Eric. Somehow it doesn't seem important now. I can't even remember what he looks like. Oh, I have to ask Dennis . . .* but Pam was asleep.

The very next day Eric Brent drove his brand-new red convertible into the campground, horn blaring, top down.

"Oh, no!" Pam couldn't believe it. Just when she was starting to like Dennis, and—she forced her thoughts back.

"Hello, Eric." Play it cool, that's what she had to do. But Eric had other ideas. He took hold of both her hands as if he owned her or something!

"Hey, Pam, let's get out of here for a while, OK?" Eric glanced at the little group of boys who had circled his shiny car. "What are they hanging around for?"

Something inside Pam began to shrivel up. Had

Eric always been so bossy, so rude? Peter was standing by her, watching and listening. Automatically her arm dropped to the little boy's shoulders. It seemed to make her stronger.

"You want to get out of here?"

Eric's laugh was smooth and confident. "Sure. Wendy told me you were up here, marooned with a bunch of kids. I thought I'd come spring you out of jail for a day!" Had Wendy really told him that? Pam doubted it. Wendy would have received her letter telling how much she liked camp. She wouldn't have passed on to Eric that Pam hated it! He was making it all up to impress her.

Out of the corner of her eye, Pam saw Dennis running across the field to get her. They were going to take a hike. When he saw her talking to Eric, his eyes traveled over the glossy surface of the new red car. Then he stopped. Shrugging his shoulders, he turned around and walked off. What must he think?

Eric was getting impatient. "Don't just stand there, get in! It's a long drive up here. I want to take you out for a spin and get back to Seattle. I've got a date tonight."

At one time Pam would have been filled with jealousy. Now she couldn't have cared less.

"Then you'd better not wait to take me out. I'm busy."

Eric really stared at her this time. This wasn't the Pam Jones who had eagerly listened to everything he had to say a few weeks ago. What had happened to her? Despite his annoyance, his interest began to grow. She sure had turned him down! He made more of an effort to be nice.

"Come on, Pam. We'll just take a little ride. I *did* come all the way up here to see you."

Pam hesitated. Eric really had made a long trip. Maybe she should go with him. Pam turned to Peter. "I won't be gone long. Then we'll go for that walk with Dennis."

Peter's face fell, but he trotted behind her as she went around the car and slid in. Eric didn't offer to open the door; he just waited for her to get in.

Pam looked at the little boy, then turned to Eric. "Could we take Peter with us?"

He scowled, then looked at Peter, who was leaning against the side of the car. "Absolutely not! Get your dirty hands off my new car, kid!"

Peter jumped back as if he had been hit. For one moment his eyes met Pam's. But Eric wasn't through yelling. He was angry at Pam for being so reluctant to go with him and at himself for wasting time driving up to this place anyway, so he took it out on Peter. "Just what are you trying to do, anyway?"

Peter's face turned white, but Eric's got red and angrier than ever. "Why don't you answer me, you dumb kid?"

It was too much. Pam, who had been trying to get words out, leaped out of the car and shouted at Eric, "You're the one who's dumb. He wasn't hurting your stupid car!" She saw Peter turn and run toward his cabin. Good. Dennis was there. He'd look after

Peter until she could get rid of Eric.

Pam had never been so angry in her whole life. "That little kid can't talk, and you come up here with your fancy car and make him feel worse! Is your paint job so precious it won't take washing? What if it did get a little dirt on it?"

Some of Eric's anger wore off. "Sorry. Let's get out of here."

Pam could barely speak. She was close to tears. She finally managed to get out, "I wouldn't ride with you from here to the main gate!"

Eric saw Pam meant what she said. "Thanks a lot. I come clear up here to take you out, and this is what I get. It will be a long time before you see me again!"

"If I never see you again in my whole life, it will be just fine with me!"

Eric jumped in his car, started the motor, and took off with a roar, throwing gravel behind and leaving Pam standing there hating him. How could she ever have liked Eric? What a great guy he had turned out to be! Eric wasn't worth worrying over. The first thing she had to do was find Peter—and find him fast. Could she undo the harm Eric had done? Or would it ruin all the progress she and Dennis had made with Peter this summer?

Pam was almost sobbing as she ran down the rows of cabins and pounded on the door of the one Dennis and Peter lived in. Dennis came to the door and opened it. She could see how cool he was to her, even before he asked, "Need something, Pam?"

"Have you seen Peter? Is he in the cabin?"

Dennis' eyes opened wide, his coolness toward Pam gone. "Why, no. Should he be?"

The tears spilled down Pam's cheeks. "I hoped he'd be here."

Dennis remembered that flashy red car and turned icy again. "Any special reason?"

"Yes. That hateful Eric—all Peter did was lean on the car, and—" How could she go on? How could she tell Dennis how awful Eric had been? She finished lamely, "He hurt Peter's feelings."

Dennis gripped Pam's shoulders hard. "Just what did your friend in the fancy car say to Peter?"

Pam didn't even notice the sarcasm. But she couldn't keep her feelings back. All her fury was in her voice as she answered, "He isn't my friend, not any longer! If I'd known what he was like, he never would have been!" She felt Dennis's fingers relax a bit.

"He called Peter dumb because Peter didn't answer when he yelled at him. I wouldn't have answered, either, the way he talked! But Peter just sort of crawled into his shell and ran off. I hoped he'd come back to his cabin!"

Now Dennis looked worried. "We've got to find him, Pam. If he's upset, there's no telling where he's gone!"

An hour later Pam and Dennis stood in front of Mr. Grayson's office. Pam was scared. How could they tell the friendly camp director what had happened? But they had to. They had looked everywhere for Peter. He just wasn't around. They had tried the campfire spot, the edge of the lake, and had even gone part way into the woods, but Dennis told her they had to report before going farther.

"Mr. Grayson, Peter's lost!" Pam blurted.

The director lost his smile and stood up. "How did that happen? The boys know they are never to leave the grounds without a counselor. Peter's never given us any trouble before."

Quickly Pam told Mr. Grayson everything, how Peter had been frightened and ashamed when Eric yelled. She ended by saying, "It's all my fault. If I hadn't gotten in the car, it wouldn't have happened."

Mr. Grayson's voice was gentle. "Don't blame yourself too much, Pam. Remember how you've helped Peter since you came." He caught her look of surprise. "Yes, I've noticed the change in him. We'll find Peter, Pam." He looked out the door. The sunshiny day had grown dark. Thunderclouds were rolling up. "I only hope we find him before it storms. It could be terrifying for him to be out alone in it."

Pam gasped and clutched Dennis' arm. He put his hand over hers and said, "We'll find him, Pam. Don't worry."

But the clouds got darker, and the rain began to pour as the counselors and older boys searched. Lightning flashed. Thunder cracked and roared. The search parties came back in, all except Dennis and Pam, who refused to stop, and Mr. Grayson's team of counselors. The boys were sent to shower and dry off while the staff searched. Where was Peter Piper?

Chapter Seven

When Eric Brent had yelled at Peter, all the little boy wanted to do was get away. He had been standing there when Pam asked if he could go for a ride, too. His eyes had glistened. To ride in a car like that, with Pam! But when Eric started yelling, Peter felt as if the world had broken off under his feet.

As Peter ran toward his cabin, away from Eric's hateful voice, he heard the car door slam and Pam saying something to Eric. Was she going with him? What difference did it make? Pam had been his friend. Now she was in that red car, ready to ride away with the boy who yelled.

Just before Peter got to his cabin, he saw Dennis step inside. He didn't want to be with anyone, not even Dennis. Something in his stomach felt funny, like he was going to be sick. He swerved away from the cabins and ran past the little chapel, past the big dining hall, up the trail to the cross. When he got there, he stopped for a minute and looked around. It was quiet. There wasn't anyone there except a rabbit and a squirrel.

Then he heard a noise in the bushes, and his eyes got big. Was that boy coming after him to yell some more? Peter took off again, up the trail, until it ended in a dim path. Still he kept on. At last he could go no farther into the undergrowth. The tangle was so dense that the branches settled back in place, making a little room all his own. That big boy couldn't find him here. No one could find him.

For the second time, Peter smiled, but there was no one there to see him except a little bird. For a long time Peter lay still, so still the little bird came closer. Peter didn't want to think about that Eric, so he thought about Pam. Pam, who had come to be his friend. Was she still his friend? Or had she gone away with the boy in the red car?

The afternoon was warm, and under here it was even warmer. Tired from his run and his tears, Peter's eyes closed, opened, and closed again. He slept so deeply he never heard when the thunder started or the rain began. The thick shrubbery protected him, even from the rain, and muffled the thunder. Peter didn't even hear when Dennis and Pam ran up the path and shouted his name. He was too worn out.

It wasn't until late afternoon that Peter awoke. He sat up, afraid. What was that awful noise? Crack! Crash! Boom! Rubbing the sleep from his eyes, he tried to figure out where he was. Vaguely he remembered running, running, running. Then it all came back to him. The red car. The big Eric, who called him names. The long run, and finally crawling into this private hideaway.

Peter stretched and started to wriggle out of his little room, but when he poked his nose out, he saw the awful storm. It was pouring rain. The thunder was still crashing and lightning flashing. He was scared. He let the branches drop and crawled back inside. His teeth chattered from the cold. With the rain and storm, the temperature had dropped.

What should he do? He was so cold! If only Pam would come get him! He huddled back against the tangled brush and tried to keep warm. At least it was dry under here. But he was so afraid. He opened his mouth to cry for Pam, but the words wouldn't come. Yet in Peter's heart and mind he was crying, along with the big tears, *Please, Pam, come and find me. You said you were my friend. Please, come get me!*

Dennis and Pam had gone back to the dining hall to see if there was any sign of Peter. There wasn't. Even Mr. Grayson's team hadn't found him.

Pam turned and ran back out in the storm. She had to find Peter. When Dennis caught up with her, she couldn't hold back her despair. "What are we going to do, Dennis? We've looked everywhere. Where can he be?"

"I know what I'm going to do." Dennis nodded at the little chapel. "I'm going in there and ask for help to find Peter." It was too much for Pam. All the heartache, the guilt over Eric, the long hours of searching came together.

"What good is that going to do? Why did God let Peter get lost? What kind of God is He, anyway?"

Dennis lost his temper. He was just as worried as Pam, and it didn't help for her to act like this. "Why don't you quit blaming God for everything that happens? It wasn't God who got Peter lost, it was your dear friend Eric Brent. I'm sick and tired of people who go around crying that God does this and that when it's usually their own fault!" If he hadn't been so upset, Dennis would never have said it.

Pam whirled toward him. "Dennis Kincaid, you're the most hateful person I know! It isn't *my* fault Peter's lost!"

"Oh? Just who did Eric come to see?"

Pam's tears of fury mingled with the streaming rain. "I hate you, Dennis Kincaid!"

Dennis didn't answer, just marched over to the door of the miniature chapel and disappeared inside. Pam stood outside in the rain, too miserable to do anything, even move. She was too proud to go in and apologize to Dennis. She was too upset to go to the trailer for dry clothing. Maybe she'd catch cold and get pneumonia. Dennis would be sorry then.

But in the middle of Pam's anger was something else. She'd never known a boy like Dennis. He really believed that God would help them find Peter. If only she could believe it too! On impulse she pushed open the door. Dennis was kneeling, head bowed. She knew he was praying. "Dennis," Pam's voice sounded small in the silent room. There was no anger in his face as he turned to her. "Dennis, if I promised God that I'll accept His Son—if I said I'd serve Him—would it help find Peter?"

Dennis stared at her. "Pam, you can't make deals with God. He wants you to accept the Lord Jesus Christ as your personal Saviour more than anything else in the world, but you can't bargain with God. You have to do it because you want to, not to help find Peter."

Pam swallowed a big lump of disappointment. "I just thought it might help—"

"We'll find Peter." There was total assurance in Dennis' voice. "Come on."

The other teams had reassembled and were heading for the beach and the campfire area. Dennis and Pam said they'd go back up the trail.

"If anything happens to Peter, I'll never get over it!" Dennis' hand should have been cold from the rain. Instead it was warm as he reached for Pam's.

"Don't blame yourself. If it hadn't been this, it could have been something else. There's always someone to make fun of a kid who's different. You know, it's amazing the way the kids have accepted Peter this summer, when he doesn't talk. It's because he's with you so much. They all like you, Pam, and so they also like Peter."

"If I could only believe that." Pam and Dennis had to walk single file now; they were back where the trail became just a path. "We were here before, Dennis. Is there any use to go farther?"

In answer, Dennis threw back his head and called, "Peter! Peter!" For a long moment there was silence; then a rustling came from the bushes. Pam and Dennis looked around. Maybe it was only a rabbit or a squirrel. But it was no rabbit or squirrel whose head poked out.

"Peter!" Pam ran to him. She noticed his quick look behind her as he pulled back. Was he afraid of her? Suddenly she knew what was wrong with him. His eyes were dull, the way they had been when she first came to camp. There was the same look in them. She hugged him hard. "Peter, he's gone. Eric's gone, in his old red car!"

Peter didn't respond. Pam knew that what she said and did right then would make all the difference in the life of this strange little boy who was locked in his own world of silence. Was all the good she had done to be lost, perhaps forever, because of Eric's cruel words? Without even knowing it, Pam's mind sent up a quick prayer for help, an automatic please-help-me-say-the-right-thing kind of prayer.

"Peter, Eric isn't my friend, ever again. You're my friend. If I'd known how awful he could be, he would *never* have been my friend!" Pam squeezed hard on Peter's thin hand. He looked at them for a long time, then at Pam. "After you left, I told him that *he* was the dumb one and that I never wanted to see him again, not ever!"

Peter didn't feel cold anymore. Pam really was his friend. She had sent that big boy in the red car away. She didn't like him. Peter could feel Pam's arms around him. It felt good. It was almost like coming home! Peter felt warm and happy. Pam couldn't know this. She only knew when he was no longer stiff. Then the little hand came up and patted Pam's cheek. Peter's eyes began to sparkle.

Dennis had held back, knowing it was up to Pam. Now he came over to them and laughed. "Hey, old man! How'd you get through this storm and not get wet? The only place you're wet is where Pam grabbed you!"

Peter almost smiled. Pam's heart went racing. They hadn't lost what they'd gained with Peter. But he was pulling her hand, getting down on his hands and knees, motioning them to follow. The three of them crawled back into the underbrush, to the little room Peter had found.

"So this is where you were. No wonder you didn't hear us when we called. You can hardly hear the thunder; even the rain doesn't get in!" Dennis grinned.

Pam knew what he was thinking. She hadn't forgotten how he went in the little chapel before they came hunting again. They *had* found Peter. It was something else to think about when she had time.

"We've got to get back to camp." Dennis swung Peter to his shoulders. Peter drooped a little. Now that the storm was over, now that Pam had found him, and now that Eric was gone, the little boy was tired and hungry. It would be good to get back to camp.

"We've got him!" Pam ran ahead to tell everyone.

Her wet face shone. Mr. Grayson saw the look of love in it and exclaimed, "Thank God!"

With happy tears in her eyes, Pam ran to her mother. "Peter was all curled up under a thick tangle of brush, way back under the branches. He didn't even get wet until we got him out of there!"

When Dennis came in with Peter on his shoulders, all the boys stood up and clapped. Then, for the first time, Peter smiled so all of them could see! His eyes shone, and when they gave him a supper tray, he ate more than he had all summer! Or so it seemed.

Pam stumbled out the door, all excited. As usual, Dennis was close behind her. They had to change before they could eat.

"He smiled, he really smiled, Dennis!"

"I know." They were on their way to the trailer but when they passed the little chapel, Pam stopped, trying to speak casually. "I think I'll just stop in here."

Dennis didn't say anything, but the big smile that came to his face said it all. He waved and went on to his own cabin to get out of his wet clothes.

The chapel was dry and warm when Pam went in. Other than that time with Dennis, she had avoided it. Now she wondered why. It was peaceful. The lighted candles flickered, showing the picture of Christ clearly.

Pam couldn't say any words out loud. But her heart was full of things she wanted to say. She wanted to say she had been wrong. She wanted to say "Thank You" for finding Peter—but the words

78

stuck in her throat. When she did speak, it was in a whisper. "I still can't accept You the way Dennis says. I don't know enough. But I want to."

Pam stayed a long time in the little chapel, but no more words would come. At last she stood up and went out quietly. But all the time she got ready for bed she thought, *Funny. I couldn't say much. But I think He understands.*

The strain of the day had been too much. Long before Mom came in from her chores Pam lay asleep, more relaxed than she had been since she first came to Sandwich Island.

Chapter Eight

Peter had been Pam's shadow ever since she got to Sandwich Island. Now that she had come for him in the storm, he stayed even closer to her. Once she tried to put in words how she felt and told Dennis, "I never knew how great it would be to have a little brother. Only children really miss something."

Dennis nodded. "I know. If I'd had brothers and sisters, it wouldn't have been so hard when we moved."

Pam looked at him curiously. "Are you going to stay where you are now?"

Dennis grinned. "No, we're just renting. Dad and Mom are talking about maybe buying a house in Seattle. How'd you like it if we moved to your neighborhood?"

Pam could feel her face get red. "I might be able to stand it." She jumped to her feet. "Come on. It's almost the end of rest period. Peter will be waiting to go with me to the story hour."

Dennis laughed at her. "Along with about 20 other boys!"

Pam spun around and grinned at Dennis. "Isn't it neat? But I still don't know how to end my story. We just *have* to catch the food bandit soon!"

It was true. Summer had been racing by, and in just a few days some of the boys would leave. Pam had to come up with a story ending before that. Every night she thought she'd go watch the kitchen storeroom door, but she always fell asleep first!

As Pam and the boys came back from the campfire circle after her story time, Mr. Grayson called her. He was standing in the door of his office. Mom, Dennis, and Mrs. Grayson were also there. What was wrong? She could see how serious they all looked.

"We've learned some bad news, Pam." Mr. Grayson held up a letter. "Peter Piper's aunt isn't getting along very well. His uncle has decided they should close their home and move into a retirement center, where they can both get proper food and care. But he's terribly worried about Peter. We aren't saying anything to Peter until we can see about finding a place for him. We know you think so much of him . . ."

Pam lost the rest of Mr. Grayson's words. She felt as if someone had hit her in the stomach. A place for Peter? Somewhere she'd probably never see him again? For a minute she thought she was going to get sick. Then it came, the big idea! She didn't even realize she had interrupted Mr. Grayson. "*We'll* adopt Peter."

She ignored Mom's exclamation, "Pam!"

Her big idea was gaining speed like a rock rolling downhill. "Why not? I've always wanted a little brother. He's just like one already. He loves me, and I—" her voice trembled, then steadied. "I love him too."

There was stone-cold, dead silence in the room. Dennis stared at her. Mr. and Mrs. Grayson stared at her. Mom stared hardest of all. "But, Pam, we can't just adopt a little boy!"

"Why not?" Pam was ready to fight. "No one else wants him. We can give him a good home."

Mom was shaking her head, but Mr. Grayson said, "Why don't we all just think and pray about Peter?"

Before Pam could hold back the words, they just blurted themselves out. "Do you really think that would help?" She clapped her hand over her mouth, but it was too late.

Mr. Grayson seemed to understand. "Yes, Pam, I do. God loves Peter very much. That's why He sent you here this summer." Long after Pam and her mother left the office and made their way to the little trailer, Pam remembered what he'd said.

"Why can't we adopt Peter, Mom? He'd love it, and so would we. I can help take care of him and everything."

Mom looked sad. "Pam, I have learned to love Peter Piper just as you do. But adopting him is out of the question. I have to be away at work all day, teaching. You're in junior high and will have activities. Who's going to look out for Peter until I get home?"

Pam had an answer to every question. "I will. I don't care about any old activities. I'd much rather have Peter."

Finally Mom said, "We just can't, Pam."

But she didn't see Pam's stubborn look. Pam had made up her mind, and that was it. She didn't know how, but surely she could talk Mom into it. Her mind raced ahead, seeing the day Peter would feel loved—and would talk.

I wonder if Mr. Grayson could be right. The thought startled Pam, but the next minute she tiptoed out of the trailer and crossed to the little chapel. When she went in, she felt sort of funny. Not so much as before she and Dennis had found Peter that stormy day, but kind of nice-funny. She sat down on a little bench, but instead of saying a real prayer, she just closed her eyes and talked out loud to God.

"You know I haven't talked to You very much for a long time, except to say thanks for finding Peter. God, if we could have Peter in our family, it would help fill up the empty space. He wouldn't ever take Daddy's place, but at least we'd be a family again. Do You suppose You could fix things so we can have him?"

Pam sat alone so long that she was late for supper. Dennis and Peter looked at her when she came to the seat they'd saved for her.

"What did you do, fall asleep?" Peter watched Pam as she laughed at Dennis' question.

"No, I was just late." Pam couldn't tell even Dennis how she'd asked God to let Peter be her brother. Instead she started eating, saying how good everything was. But after supper, Dennis sent Peter to the cabin to get a jacket, and asked Pam, "Did your mom change her mind?"

"Not yet. Dennis, do you think she will? Do you think she might let us adopt him?"

"I don't know. Pam, I'm not sure it would be the best thing for Peter."

"What!" Pam could feel her temper rising. "You said yourself Peter loves me more than he does anyone else."

Dennis was patient, but he still shook his head. "It's not that. He does love you. But what about growing up without a father?"

Pam drooped. That was unfair. Dennis took hold of her hand. "I'm not trying to be mean, Pam. But you know how much you miss your own dad, and you had him with you until just a little while ago. What if you'd never had him?"

"That's different. Peter's father died a long time ago."

"I know. But if a family with both a father and mother took Peter, he could grow up more complete. A boy needs a dad, Pam."

Pam felt hot tears in her eyes. She wouldn't admit it, but maybe Dennis was right. To cover up her feelings she said, "I suppose someone will get Peter, and I'll never even see him again. I could make up to Peter for not having a dad."

"I have an idea—" Before he could say any more Peter came running up to them.

I wonder what Dennis' idea is? All through camp-fire Pam wondered. When it was over, there was no time to talk. Peter was with them, as usual, as they climbed the hill back to the main level of the camp. The stars were bright and big. It was warm, and a little breeze blew in from the water.

"Good night for the camp bandit to strike again." Dennis didn't know Peter's ears had caught the low whisper. He didn't see Peter's eyes get bigger. Ever since the big storm, Peter had looked rested. But tonight . . .

Pam had been sound asleep when she heard a voice at the window above her head. It scared her, and she sat up in bed. The hands of the travel alarm pointed to 12. Who could be whispering through her window at midnight? She snatched a robe and leaned closer to the window.

"Pam, wake up." It was Dennis. Something must be terribly wrong for him to be out of his cabin in the middle of the night. Pam fumbled with the buttons and slipped out the door, noticing Mom hadn't awakened.

"Pam, have you seen Peter?"

"Seen Peter! At this hour of the night? Of course not. Don't you know what time it is?"

Dennis grunted. "Do you think I'd be here if I didn't?"

Some of his worry reached Pam, and she asked, "Peter isn't in the cabin?"

Dennis shook his head. "No. He's not in the rest room or chapel or church or dining hall. I thought maybe he'd come here."

Pam shivered. The warm night air suddenly seemed cold to her. She remembered that awful afternoon and evening of the storm, and the same cold fear made her shudder.

Pam really was worried now. There was also something in the back of her mind, if she could only remember! She closed her eyes tight, forcing herself to go back over the day. She had it! When she'd been telling about the further adventures of the food bandit that day, she'd noticed the funniest expression on Peter's face. She hadn't thought much of it then, but now—

"Dennis, when did you miss him?"

"About a half hour ago. I thought I heard the door creak. The boys know they aren't supposed to get up in the night without telling one of their counselors. We've never had any trouble on the grounds, but we don't take any chances. If someone needs to go to the bathroom, one of us goes with him.

"Anyway, I looked around and everything seemed to be OK. I almost went back to sleep, then I remembered how rumpled the blankets in Peter's bunk were. So I got up, and he was gone. I checked all the usual places before coming here."

"Dennis, if he got out without being caught this time, could he have done it before?" In the light from the big post lamp, Pam could see the look on Dennis's face.

"You mean . . ."

Pam nodded. "I hate to think it, but maybe, just maybe, Peter's the one who's been taking the food."

"That's impossible!"

"I hope so." But deep inside Pam could feel that same sick feeling. What if Peter were the thief? She couldn't bear it!

It was all Pam could do to keep up with Dennis as they rounded the corner of the kitchen storeroom. She was frantically sending up a little prayer to a God she was just beginning to trust again: *Please, don't let it be Peter.* The next moment she nearly cried.

There, holding an apple, was Peter.

Chapter Nine

Pam's world went dark. All her disappointment showed in her voice as she said, "Oh, Peter, how could you?" He looked so small and scared standing there. A great wave of anger crashed over Pam. How could God let such things happen? How could He let Peter be a thief?

Dennis knelt down on the ground and looked right at Peter. "All right, old man, why did you do it?" Peter's eyes got bigger than ever. For one moment Dennis and Pam thought he was going to speak. His mouth opened, but no words came. He only shook his head, again and again, and looked at Pam. Big tears flooded his eyes . . . and something else. He looked as if he were asking her to understand, to be his friend. Then he shook his head again.

Pam's heart gave a big bounce. Her voice was excited as she dropped down beside Peter and Dennis. "Dennis, I think he's telling us he didn't take the apples. I think he's saying he isn't the food thief!"

Peter's face lit up. For the second time, he smiled—a great big smile—and nodded his head up and down as hard as he could. Pam was so glad she didn't know what to do. All she could think of was to hug Peter hard and say, "I believe you, Peter. I don't know why you're here in the middle of the night with that apple, but I do believe that you didn't steal it."

Her eyes met Dennis' eyes squarely, noting the little doubt there. But he only said, "Come on, old man, back to bed with you."

There was no time for Dennis and Pam to talk. It wasn't the time or place. He had to get Peter back to the cabin before they were missed. But the next day they would have to take Peter to Mr. Grayson. Pam tossed and turned, unable to get back to sleep. Finally she dozed off. She dreamed Peter was being sent away from camp in disgrace. All the boys were pointing their fingers and calling Peter a thief! When she awakened, she didn't feel rested. She just felt scared about what might happen to Peter. What would Mr. Grayson do? Well, she'd stick up for Peter! She really believed he hadn't taken the apples. And yet, there were all those times when he had seemed so exhausted. If he'd been out much of the night, he would have been tired.

Pam felt that her head was one big squirrel cage, with all the thoughts running around inside it. Nothing was said in front of the other boys about the midnight raid. But late in the morning Dennis, Peter, and Pam went to see the camp director.

Mr. Grayson listened to the whole story, his kind

eyes never leaving Peter's face. If Peter were guilty, he hid it well! There was an anxious—but not a guilty—look on his face. Mr. Grayson took Peter on his lap and asked him, "Peter, did you take the apples?"

Peter shook his head, his eyes full of tears. Even though there wasn't any other explanation, Pam and Dennis believed the little boy. Dennis had lain awake too. He had decided there was no way in the world Peter could be a thief.

Mr. Grayson believed Peter. "I believe you, Peter. You may go."

Peter's eyes shone as he slid off Mr. Grayson's lap. Before he went out, he turned and looked toward Pam. Again she saw that look, asking for understanding. Then he opened his mouth. With all his might, he tried to speak. The other three in the room held their breath. If only Peter could say something!

Peter tried again, then again. On the third try, a little squeak came out of the throat he hadn't used for so long. And then, "Ban . . . dit!" He got the word out, then turned and ran through the door, leaving the others wondering whether they had really heard him!

Pam's face fell. "Oh, no! What have I done with my bandit story?" Peter must have thought he could help her. Some of the thrill of hearing him speak for the first time in years was lost in worry over what was happening. She said, "I've made a mess of everything!" Tears started to spill from her eyes.

"Daddy asked me to take care of Mom, and I haven't done that. I love Peter, but Mom says it isn't fair to adopt him, because she can't be home. Now the story I've told the boys has gotten Peter in trouble. Everything I've tried to do has gone wrong!"

Mr. Grayson caught Dennis' eye and motioned toward the door. Pam didn't even notice when he left. Suddenly she needed someone to talk with, a man, like Daddy. It all spilled out. "Just before he died, Daddy asked me to take care of Mom. But I'm not strong enough. I tried to write a story and earn some money. It wasn't any good. Why did my dad have to die?"

Mr. Grayson just let Pam cry. It would heal her. When she finally mopped her eyes, he looked across the table at Pam. His voice was kind and understanding. "We never have an answer to those questions, Pam, not in this life. To us it seems cruel for God to let our loved ones die. Yet we know we'll someday see them again."

Pam felt miserable. "I know. I try so hard, Mr. Grayson." She told him how she had felt before she came, then how she had just started to feel maybe God did care about her, even if Dad was gone. "I thought maybe He'd let me have Peter instead. Now that won't even happen."

Mr. Grayson leaned forward. He knew of what Dennis had told Pam about Peter needing a father. "Pam, would you really want to keep Peter, if you knew he'd be better off with a family where there's a father?"

It was a hard question. Pam sat still, just thinking, for a long, long time. She thought of how Peter sat close to her. She thought of how much she loved him. Could she give him up? Then she thought of the way she had loved Dad, and how she'd felt since he was gone—kind of lost and left behind.

Pam shook her head. "No, I guess not." They were the hardest words she ever had to say.

Mr. Grayson beamed. "Good. I think the Kincaids have made arrangements for Peter to be adopted into a real family, one with a father, a mother, and an older brother. Peter needs a family, Pam—a whole family. This mother stays at home and can be with him." He stopped, then went on, his voice quiet. "Pam, I have to tell you, you have helped Peter at this point in his life more than anyone else in the world could have done. You were sent here to help him, I know that. I've watched him open up from being a hurting little child to one who trusts you. Do you think he would have spoken if it hadn't been for you?"

Pam had to be honest. "I don't know."

Mr. Grayson smiled at her and stood up. "I do, Pam. Now run along and see if you can get Peter to say anything else." She was almost out the door when Mr. Grayson added, "Pam, don't think you aren't helping your mother. She told me you didn't want to come here. But the way you've handled Peter has made her happier than she's been since your dad died." He cleared his throat. "She also accepted the Lord as her personal Saviour at staff devotions this morning. She'll tell you later today when she isn't so busy, but I thought it might help to know now."

Pam scuffed her shoes along the gravel path as she went to find Peter. So Mom had accepted Jesus. Why did that make her feel so good and yet so alone all at the same time? But when she saw Peter on a rock waiting for her, it slipped from her mind.

"Ban . . . dit. Ban . . . dit. Ban . . . dit." Peter's eyes shone. He jumped up and down. He saw her old black scarf with the holes in it hanging out of her jeans pocket and snatched it out, putting it over his eyes. Then he danced around saying, "Ban . . . dit. Ban . . . dit."

Pam stared at him. Her heart sank. It was just a game to Peter, a big game she'd started during her first story hour. She didn't believe Peter had taken the apples, but how could she prove it? His hopping all over the place with a mask over his face and shouting "Ban . . . dit" wasn't going to help!

While the younger boys were swimming that afternoon, Pam and Dennis had a long talk.

"I think I know why Peter was up there," Pam said. "He must have heard me telling you I wished we could catch the food bandit so I could end my story. He must have decided to go wait and see who came. That would explain how tired he was and how he fell asleep every night right away. He must have slipped out later."

Dennis agreed. "He wanted to be your friend. He knows friends are people who help each other. You even said something like that one day. He's always around you, popping out of nowhere. It's his way of doing what he could for his friend."

"That makes me feel just awful! What if we can't prove he didn't take things?"

"Mr. Grayson believes Peter. Things will work out, Pam. If nothing more is taken, then—" Dennis shrugged. "We'll worry about it when it happens. I'll keep an extra-close watch on Peter, put him in the bunk above mine. There'll be no way he can get out without waking me."

"I just hope things keep disappearing!"

But for the next two nights, nothing was taken. Had Peter been lying after all? Pam kept asking her mother so much about the food that Mom finally said, "Why so interested? Do you want a job in the kitchen?"

Pam couldn't tell her what it was all about. Mr. Grayson had asked her and Dennis not to discuss Peter with anyone.

Monday morning Dennis rushed up to Pam in the breakfast line. "Want to see you as soon as you're done eating." She could hardly wait to eat. Dennis was really acting mysterious! She gobbled her food and ran outside. He looked both ways to be sure no one was around, then said, "More apples disappeared last night—and Peter wasn't out of the cabin!"

Before she thought, Pam threw her arms around him. "That's wonderful!"

Dennis roared with laughter.

"I don't care! It *is* wonderful. It means Peter was telling the truth!"

"I know. I just had to give you a bad time." Dennis' cockiness got through to her. If only she could show Dennis how much this meant to her! Suddenly an idea hit her. If Peter could spy, then so could she. The food thief might strike again, that very night. Well, this time, she'd be hidden behind the big tree, just the way her story said.

"Who can it be? Why did Peter call the thief 'ban-dit'?" Dennis couldn't get over his gladness that Peter was not guilty.

"I don't know." But Pam didn't tell Dennis that maybe, just maybe, she *would* know, and soon!

It was almost midnight when Mom's soft breathing told Pam she was asleep. Shoes in hand, Pam slipped outside, noticing how quiet and peaceful it was. The little chapel gleamed white in the soft light, and as she passed it, Pam almost stopped. Instead, she smiled and went on. She'd stop on the way back, if everything went right.

Quietly Pam crept to the big tree, keeping her hand over her mouth to keep back laughter. Just like Nancy Drew, creeping around in the night to solve mysteries! For a long time nothing happened. She started to get sleepy. Then—she heard a soft stir in the bushes. Someone or something was there.

Pam's sleepiness suddenly disappeared. She leaned forward, trying to see. Someone, or something, was crawling along the ground. She could hear it against the fir needles on the ground. Why was she here, anyway? All kinds of horrible stories went through her mind.

For a moment Pam almost turned and left. But the memory of Peter's little face haunted her, and she bit her lip. She had to stay! She crept forward for a better look at the storeroom door. It was still shut—and locked. But above it and to the left was a small window that was left open for ventilation. Suddenly a bright ray of moonlight shot straight toward the window. Peter had been right. There wriggling through it was a bandit, masked, in the moonlight. He was holding an apple just as Peter had! Pam couldn't believe her eyes. Now that she had actually seen the thief she was no longer afraid. She was *glad* she had come. Peter had been telling the truth.

As Pam passed the little chapel on her way back to the trailer, she stepped inside. She couldn't stay long, but there was something she had to do. At first she sat down on the little bench but then knelt on the floor.

"Dear God, I've tried to make all kinds of deals with You. Dennis says it doesn't work. I know now he's right." Pam took a deep breath. Her voice trembled. "I'm sorry, God—for everything. You found Peter, and You helped me find out he was telling the truth. I've been stubborn. Dennis was right. I've rebelled against You. No more. I'm not very good material, but please, come into my heart and help me live the way You want.

"One more thing, God. Whatever's best for Peter will be OK with me. I don't want to fight with You any longer. I just want You to be my friend—and my Saviour." Two bright tears sparkled in the light from the candles. The same warm feeling that had gone through her before crept over her again. Her fight was over—and she had the answer to more mysteries than one! Jesus would be with her forever, and Peter would be proved a hero in a few days.

Chapter Ten

It was time for the story hour. As usual, Peter was right by Pam's side. She looked down at her boys, all so different, all waiting. How she loved them! What if she had never come to Sandwich Island, and met them and Dennis—and found Jesus and God? She shivered a little in the sunny air.

"Tell us the end of the bandit story, Pam," Butch teased. "We're going home tomorrow, at least some of us." It was true. Summer was almost over.

"All right." Pam held up her hands to stop the clapping. "But first I want to tell you another story." She saw the disappointed looks. Her hands felt cold, but she had to do it. "At church services and camp-fires you've heard a lot about God and how He sent His Son Jesus to earth because He loved us so much." She took a deep breath. "Before I came here, I knew about God and Jesus. But I learned I didn't know Them personally. I had never accepted Jesus as my Saviour or asked Him to come into my life. I didn't want to come here. I was afraid I wouldn't have a good time this summer."

Pam looked around at the rows of eager faces, then smiled reassuringly and hugged Peter. "I just want to say that my mom and I have both accepted Jesus as our Saviour. We're saved." She wasn't prepared for the rush of talk.

"I was saved when I was 6," Butch boasted.

"I was 8." "I was 7." It appeared most of the boys at the story hour knew all about salvation and had already accepted Christ into their hearts!

"That's wonderful!" Pam couldn't hide her excitement. "If any of you haven't accepted Him, I can tell you it's great." Her smile faded a little, thinking of how she would be losing Peter. "He doesn't promise never to let us have trouble. But He does make it easier to deal with trouble." Her voice trembled. She hadn't thought she could say it out loud. "I lost my dad in a terrible accident not too long ago, and it's still hard. He can't come back, but I'm going to trust God, and I know that someday I'll see my dad again."

The boys sat quietly, thinking. Even small Peter was serious, his newfound smile missing as he listened intently.

"Now, who knows what a hero is?" Pam broke the little silence that had fallen. She had given her testimony, given the boys a chance to think about it. She had also seen Dennis a little way off in the trees as they had planned. He hadn't been able to cover the big grin that spread across his face as she told of meeting the Lord and accepting Him.

"I do." "I know what a hero is!" But it was Butch who blurted out, "He's the good guy!"

Pam laughed again. "Do you know Peter is a hero, a real hero?" Everyone looked at Peter. He didn't look like he used to. He wasn't as thin or pale or sober. He was happy and strong and smiled a lot.

"How come Peter's a hero?" Butch demanded.

It was here, the moment Pam had waited for so long. "Because the bandit story is really true. We had a food bandit right here on Sandwich Island!"

The boys gasped and moved in closer to her. Pam made her voice mysterious. "Peter Piper got up in the middle of the night and watched the kitchen storeroom door. He saw the bandit. He solved the mystery! A few nights later I stayed up, and I saw the bandit too. I waited and waited. Last night Dennis and I captured the bandit. *He's here right now!*"

Peter was the only boy who didn't look a little scared. Even Butch had slid closer to Pam's feet.

"Bring in the bandit!" But it was only Dennis who came, carrying a big box covered with a heavy cloth. The boys' eyes nearly popped from their heads. Dennis slowly took off the cloth. Underneath was a cage, and in the cage was—a raccoon!

"Ban . . . dit! Ban . . . dit!" The boys shouted and clapped. Not only had the food bandit been discovered, Peter Piper was talking!

"Bandit! Raccoon!"

"He could get in through the small window next to the door," Pam told the boys. "See, doesn't he look like a real bandit?" She pointed to the little black mask over the raccoon's eyes, just like the mask she'd made for the story. "Peter discovered him. Peter's a hero!"

"He-ro!" The boys cheered again. All summer they had played with Peter, feeling sorry for him. Now Butch held out his hand, "C'mon, Peter. Let's go tell the others about you being a hero!"

Peter took Butch's hand but turned and ran back to Pam. As he hugged her, he whispered, "Friend. Jesus," then trotted off with the other boys.

Dennis hadn't said a word, but Pam told him, "When I accepted Jesus, I told God it would be all right about—about Peter being given to a family with a father. But, oh, Dennis, it has to be a family who will teach him about God and Jesus! Just now, he said, 'Friend. Jesus.' He understands, I'm sure."

"Of course he does. We have devotions in our cabins. Peter couldn't talk, but I could tell by his eyes that he listened. I wouldn't be surprised if in his own way, in his heart, Peter has already accepted Jesus."

"It was really hard, telling God that. Like you said, what's past isn't important anymore. I have to go on. No, I have Someone to go on with me, and it's because you told me about Him."

"Pam." There was a strange note in Dennis' voice. "I've got some news that will show you you're going to have some others around to help you go on with Him."

"Who?"

"The family who plan to adopt Peter is also

102

planning to move into your neighborhood!"

Pam's eyes sparkled. She jumped up. "Really? Then I'll get to see him often!"

"Whenever you like."

"But what if those people don't want me to come over? What if they don't like me and won't let me visit Peter?"

"They will."

But Pam couldn't keep back her new fear. "How do you know?"

"The family adopting Peter is named Kincaid. They have a father, a mother, an older brother, and . . ." He never got a chance to finish.

"You? You're adopting Peter? Then God knew it all along." Surprise weakened Pam's knees, and she dropped to a fallen log.

"Of course. He always knows what's best for His children." Dennis turned red. "Sorry, didn't mean to preach."

"Why didn't you tell me sooner?"

"I couldn't," Dennis confessed. "You had to come to God in your own way, of your own free will, not just as a 'Thank You.'"

Pam remembered when she'd thought of doing just that, of bribing God to find Peter. But Dennis continued, "Dad was gone a couple of days this week. We're buying a house in Seattle that used to belong to a family named Brent. They have a son named Eric, who, they said, was going to go back east to a 'good school.'"

Eric Brent moving away? Dennis and his family moving in—with Peter?

"I don't deserve all this."

"We never deserve the things God sends us, Pam. But if we trust Him, it happens just as the Bible says—all things work together for good, for those who love the Lord." He cleared his throat. It was hard for him to talk like this. "I guess He just wants us to trust Him, even in hard times, to come through. He always does." The next minute he reached down and pulled Pam up. "Come on. You'll be late for supper."

The Kincaids thought Pam and her mother should be with them when they told Peter about his aunt and uncle and his new home. After supper they all walked up the woodsy trail and sat down on logs by the clearing with the cross. Dennis had Peter on his lap, with Pam next to him, close enough for Peter to touch.

"Peter, your aunt is pretty sick, so she and your uncle have decided they must move to a retirement center. They won't have room for you there, even though they love you very much, but, Peter, how would you like to come live at our house?" Mr. Kincaid asked the little boy. Peter's eyes got big. "I would be your daddy, and my wife would be your mommy."

Dennis added, "How about it, old man? How'd you like me for a big brother?"

Everyone waited. Peter just sat there for a minute. He thought and thought and thought. Then he shook his head. The Kincaids' faces fell. They had been so sure Peter would want to come to them! Dennis really looked hurt. "Don't you want to live with us, Peter?"

Peter's eyes flashed, and he slowly slid down from Dennis's lap. He curled up at Pam's feet and took her hand, then said, "Friend." Suddenly the others understood.

"Pam will be just a few houses away, Peter. You can see her every single day!"

Peter looked at Pam. She nodded. "Yes, Peter, and you'll come over and stay with me sometimes!"

For a long time Peter just sat there. Then he got up, and went to Mr. Kincaid. "Daddy?" Mr. Kincaid nodded.

Peter trotted to Mrs. Kincaid. "Mommy?" She couldn't keep back the tears in her eyes and hugged him hard. But he broke away and went on around the circle.

"Brother?"

Dennis grinned. "You bet, old man."

Peter paused for a long time in front of Mrs. Jones. She saw he didn't know what to call her. Her voice was gentle. "I'm your Aunt Kat, Peter." He looked puzzled, then said, "Aunt Kat. Meow?" They all laughed! Peter was getting a head start on them with all his words. Pretty soon he'd be chattering away all the time.

But when Peter came back to Pam, he climbed on her lap, and said simply, "Friend."

"That's right, Peter. You're my friend, and I'm

your friend." Contented, Peter looked around the circle—and laughed! The others were happy and thankful for the change in this little boy who would now be part of both their families. Peter Piper, the little boy who didn't talk, had come a long way that summer.

That night when all was still, Pam slipped out of bed. It wasn't late, but she wanted to be alone, even away from Mom. She went to the little chapel and stepped inside. How beautiful it was, and how peaceful! She sat down on the bench and just thought for a while. There was so *much* to think about! Mom had said, when she heard the story of Peter, "Pam, you'll never know what it means to me, this summer up here." She brushed away mist from her eyes. "For both of us to find new friends, and the greatest friend of all, Jesus."

Now as Pam sat in the dim light, she felt close to Dad, even though he was gone. There would always be an empty place in her life. But she wasn't angry with God anymore. She had let His Holy Spirit start to fill the emptiness.

Dad would be proud of me, even more than Mom. For the first time Pam knew she was keeping her promise to Dad, really keeping it.

The next morning when Mom left to make breakfast, Pam didn't turn over and go back to sleep. Instead, she took out the story she had started writing so long ago back in Seattle, the story she had been so proud of writing. Her gaze flew over the paper:

"The beautiful girl heard racing footsteps behind her. Running faster, she looked back. The spy had found her out! She must escape. The secret she carried . . ."

Pam threw her head back and laughed out loud. How silly! Mrs. Johnstone had been right. What did she—Pam—know of foreign intrigue? She tossed the pages into the wastebasket and picked up her pen.

What should she write? A children's story, featuring the food bandit? A story about a raccoon? Pam's head moved slowly back and forth. No. She had learned something a lot more important this summer. She thought of the beautiful camp here on Sandwich Island. She thought of the Norwegian people who had given the land away because they felt God wanted them to. She hadn't understood when Dennis told her the story. But now she was beginning to understand.

Outside the window two squirrels scampered past. A little brown rabbit hopped by, and the birds were singing their hearts out. What if she hadn't come? Again that shiver went down her spine. Never to have had a story hour, or known Peter, or Dennis? Never to have knelt in the little chapel and felt the warmth of God's welcome filling her when she asked Jesus to come into her life? How awful!

Would she ever see the boys from story hour again, except Peter? Some of them might come back next year. Would she? Even if she did, it would be different, new boys, other staff.

"If I could only put on paper what I found up here!" Pam closed her eyes, thinking of the boys following her around the campfire circle, chanting, "I *know* I can, I *know* I can!" She could see the huge birthday cake for her thirteenth birthday and Peter's sixth birthday.

Peter! In the middle of feeling sad about leaving in a few weeks, Pam had forgotten that Peter and the Kincaids would be living just down the street from her in Seattle. She'd show Dennis around school the same way Dennis had shown her around camp. She wouldn't be introducing him to her church youth group—Mom said they were changing churches and would be going to the same church as the Kincaids. They could get acquainted together. She would introduce him to Wendy. Would Wendy understand about Pam's commitment to Christ?

Suddenly Pam knew it was terribly important for Wendy and her other friends to understand. "If I could only write it down, everything I've learned. How happiness is doing what God wants and helping others." Peter's dark eyes flashed into her memory.

Pen poised above the page, Pam's thoughts flew thick and fast. *I'll never win the **Seventeen** contest with this story. So what? If I can put down what I learned here, it will be more important than any contest in the whole world.* The pen trembled, stilled.

No matter how long I live—"Wait! That's it!" Pam's pen flew over the paper, pouring out words almost faster than she could write. When she paused to rest her hand, she read the first paragraph aloud.

"No matter how long I live, I will remember the summer of my thirteenth birthday. It started out miserable. But it ended up very differently, and all because of a red-haired boy named Dennis, who taught me to love God, and a little boy named Peter, who taught me to love other people. . . ."

Pam paused, then deliberately wrote a title in the empty space at the top of the page: *Sandwich Island Summer.* Her story would tell others what she had learned, but it would have no end. Pam knew in her heart it was only the beginning.

Also by Colleen L. Reece

Escape From Fear. A camping trip meets with disaster. Jeff must leave his injured father alone in a mountain snowstorm and find his way down a poorly marked trail in the dark. Where will he find the courage he needs? Paper, 96 pages. US$4.95, Cdn$6.20.

JumpStart! A favorite *Guide* author brings you power-packed devotionals that help you make important choices, solve problems, and work out relationships. Many devotionals are followed by a fun activity or exercise, such as a game you can play with your family or friends. Hardcover, 412 pages. US$9.95, Cdn$12.45.

The Mysterious Treadle Machine. There's something valuable hidden in Tante Theresa's old treadle machine and Terri and Tim aren't the only ones who know about it. Someone keeps trying to steal it. Only no one can find it! Join Terri and Tim for a summer at the beach filled with exciting adventures and help them solve this mystery! US$4.95, Cdn$6.20.

P.K. the Great. Through a series of adventures—and misadventures—cocky Jack discovers that the only way to be truly great is to accept the fact that he isn't the greatest—Jesus is. Paper, 96 pages. US$4.95, Cdn$6.20.

Plain, Plain Melissa Jane. Freckle-nosed Melissa Jane longs to be beautiful. A stray puppy brings her more worry, heartache, and joy than she could have dreamed possible and helps her learn something very special about beauty. Paper, 125 pages. US$4.95, Cdn$6.20.

To order, call **1-800-765-6955** or write to ABC Mailing Service, P.O. Box 1119, Hagerstown, MD 21741. Send check or money order. Enclose applicable sales tax and 15 percent (minimum US$2.50) for postage and handling. Prices and availability subject to change without notice. Add 7 percent GST in Canada.

The Shadow Creek Ranch Series
By Charles Mills

Escape to Shadow Creek Ranch. A siren's wail cuts through the cool night air. Fifteen-year-old Joey Dugan runs faster than he's ever run before. A deadly secret hides in his pocket. So begins a breathtaking adventure that frees him from the mean streets of New York City to live among the towering granite mountains of Montana with his new family. There he makes exciting discoveries about God and joins in the plans to make Shadow Creek Ranch a summer getaway for other city kids like himself.

Take the long journey to Shadow Creek Ranch. Find new meaning for your own life as you join Joey, Debbie, Wendy, Grandpa, and their friends. Watch God's creatures live and play among magnificent mountains and deep, green, valleys. Hurry! Make your reservation today! Paper, 143 pages. US$3.95, Cdn$4.95.

Mystery in the Attic. There's something hidden in the attic! Wendy insists it's a curse. Suddenly, all the inhabitants of Shadow Creek Ranch find themselves facing baffling challenges, nerve-splitting adventures. Is it the curse? Has their beloved ranch fallen victim to a power beyond their control?

Join Debbie, Joey, Wendy, and Samantha as they face a springtime mystery that is so intense it seems to place their very lives in peril, but that ultimately reveals a wonderful secret about the limitless power of God. This exciting sequel to *Escape to Shadow Creek Ranch* whisks you off to Montana to soar with the red-tailed hawk, thunder along mountain roads with Tar Boy and Early, and meet a mysterious Indian named Red Stone. Paper. US$4.95, Cdn$6.20.

To order, call **1-800-765-6955** or write to ABC Mailing Service, P.O. Box 1119, Hagerstown, MD 21741. Send check or money order. Enclose applicable sales tax and 15 percent (minimum US$2.50) for postage and handling. Prices and availability subject to change without notice. Add 7 percent GST in Canada.

More Great Stories!

The Best of *Guide* Videos. Here are six of the best stories printed
by *Guide*, brought to video with exciting sound effects and vivid
illustrations. Host Ron Pride acts out everyday experiences that
reinforce the Christian values found in each story. Each VHS
video is approximately 25 minutes in length and features three
stories. US$19.95, Cdn$24.95 each.

Once in Old Frisco. Elaine Egbert. Tired of milking cows,
weeding corn, and hearing about God, Karl goes to San Francisco
to strike it rich. But an earthquake shakes up his life and begins
to change his mind about needing God. Paper, 125 pages.
US$6.95, Cdn$8.70.

Sea Island Sanctuary. Jean Holmes. Share high adventure with
teenage Becky and Dani as they discover the secrets of a remote
island, meet the intriguing Turtle Woman, and narrowly escape
the dangers of Sneaker Sucker Swamp and Alligator Pond.
Paper, 127 pages. US$6.95, Cdn$8.70.

So Much Summer. Kris Coffin Stevenson. "This will be a special
summer, one you will remember the rest of your life." That's
what Kris's dad told her when he agreed to take her on a
geology expedition. But she wasn't counting on falling down the
slope into the rock quarry, seeing grizzly bears, or getting sick
from eating currants! Paper, 96 pages. US$6.95, Cdn$8.70.

To order, call **1-800-765-6955** or write to ABC Mailing Service, P.O. Box
1119, Hagerstown, MD 21741. Send check or money order. Enclose
applicable sales tax and 15 percent (minimum US$2.50) for postage and
handling. Prices and availability subject to change without notice. Add
7 percent GST in Canada.